To Thanks Ready! V. P. [signature] (handwritten)

GOOD BOY BEN

V P FELMLEE

Book Two of the Abandoned Trilogy.

vfauthor.com

Published by TCS Publishing

ISBN: 9798397306263

DEDICATION

Dedicated to all of the adoption and rescue organizations in the world, for all animals, for all people. Especially to the millions of wonderful fosters who perform miracles every day, caring, nurturing, healing, and helping puppies and kittens, dogs and cats, many of whom may have seen the worst of people, but now see the best, in those loving hands.

In Appreciation

Thank you to my wonderful editor Roscoe Betunada, and Kitty Nicholason and Sherry Ficklin for their enduring support and encouragement.

Also by V P Felmlee

The Amazing, Interesting, Dangerous, and Somewhat True
Adventures of Prince Tadpole & Princess Clara

CONTENTS

ACKNOWLEDGMENTS

Thank you, to all of the readers of the *Prince Tadpole & Princess Clara* book, the first in the Abandoned Trilogy. Because you asked the question, "What happens to Good Boy Ben?" his story is now in your hands.

CHAPTER ONE
THE DRY, DUSTY, HOT ROAD

It was a bad day for a big dog who found himself alone on a dry, dusty, hot road. Worse, it was windy and getting windier by the minute.

The day had begun in a usual way. That morning, his person had said, "Come on, Ben. Ready to go for a ride in the bye-bye car?"

Of course! Ben was *always* ready to go for a ride. He jumped in, tongue hanging, tail wagging. Who knew where they'd be going? It was always a wonderful surprise but he hoped they'd be going to his park, where they always had balls thrown for him to catch, and people to tell him what a handsome dog he was. And treats, lots of treats! Then back home for his breakfast, and maybe a nap.

The window rolled down. He looked over at his person, thanking him. He loved it when the window was open, he could poke his head out, feel an exhilarating rush of air into his nose and mouth. He could see and smell everything in the world. His tongue hung out and his smile was big and sloppy.

Sometime later, the car stopped and the door opened.

"Out you go, come on now," his person said. "Good boy, Ben."

Those Three Magic Words: "Good boy, Ben."

He jumped from the seat onto the road, dancing around in a full circle, wagging his tail back and forth, his heart beating with excitement.

His person threw a ball. "Go fetch!" came the command.

Oh, good, they must be at the park. The ball arced a long way, and the dog took off running as fast as he could to fetch it. He was *built* for fetching.

The ball bounced into some bushes. *This is a different park*, Ben thought as he launched into the prickly greenery, searching for the ball. There was no soft grass, and no lake where he sometimes splashed around. No little people running and playing. No big people walking or sitting. Nope, not his park.

There's the ball! Gleeful, happy as always, he grabbed it, then turned to run back to the car.

He saw it down the road, he must have run much farther than he usually did, but it was moving away. He ran faster, as fast as he could, but he couldn't catch up. The car disappeared and now the big dog saw only swirls of dirt.

The ball still in his mouth, he sauntered down the road. He looked behind him, and from side to side. He was confused. And hot. *And* thirsty.

Some water would be nice. But he couldn't smell any, which was odd. He could always smell water, outside in his yard, or in the house next to his kibble bowl.

He wandered farther and farther down the dusty road, still searching for the car and his person. Specks of dirt hurt his eyes. His long fur beat against his face. He dropped the ball and watched it bounce away.

Ben sat down, and waited.

And waited.

And waited.

And…waited…

CHAPTER TWO
DEADBEATS

Sid stood on the street corner opposite the strip mall. There were only a handful of shops, among them a shoe store, a seafood restaurant, a hair salon, and a women's clothing boutique. Sid knew women were the most likely to give him a handout while they waited in their cars for the light to change, so the corner might be a good place.

This was a new begging spot for him; the one he favored was under construction. There were others, of course, but usually they were taken very early in by other homeless people, huddled in coats and blankets in the cool morning air. The spaces were always crowded with wheeled carts, bags, boxes, and, more frequently, small dogs or puppies. He avoided them if at all possible, which was usually all of the time.

Sid didn't consider himself "homeless" as much as an ordinary "hitcher," traveling with the benefit of a stuck-out thumb from town to town, state to state. But for many, the nuanced difference was meaningless. Because he stood on street corners waiting for a handed-out dollar bill or two, he was, by any definition, homeless.

He was rewarded with some change, a fiver, even a ten, from cars stopped for the red light. Of course, there were also a dozen or so middle fingers and a few yells of "Get a job," and "Deadbeat," from young men racing by in loud trucks and SUVs. If he had a dollar for every time he heard those two expressions, he'd have enough money to buy his own car.

But today he was content with the twenty dollars in his pocket.

Now it was time to do his "grocery run." Most homeless (which, again, he shunned in both name and association), thought big stores were best, rummaging through dumpsters, pulling out spoiled fruits and vegetables, outdated cartons of milk, or half-eaten salads and sandwiches. Sid knew better. The smaller shops such as bakeries and delicatessens were much more likely to give hand-outs especially in the afternoon after closing.

Today was no exception. He showed up at a deli a few streets away at just the right time. Over the years he had developed friendships of sorts with some store owners and workers in town, including a sympathetic fellow at this deli who was shy on words but generous with leftovers. The back door was open, and Sid saw the worker through the screen. They nodded to each other; a paper bag was quickly offered before the door was shut.

Sid waited until he was a couple of streets over before looking: Four nice and thick boneless pork chops, some bagels, and four small containers of macaroni and cheese. All destined for the local landfill but instead would serve as a nice supper for ol' Sid.

It was getting close to dusk, shops were closing, and traffic picking up as people hurried home. He took back streets, avoiding subdivisions, getting on a dirt road as soon as possible to get away and disappear.

It would soon be dark.

Hurry now, hurry.

CHAPTER THREE
THIRST

Ben whined and shifted his weight on his front legs back and forth, back and forth. He didn't know what to do. Should he wait for his person? Leave here and go looking for him? He was getting thirsty and hungry. Mostly thirsty. It was so hot and the trees were stingy with their shade.

He decided to walk the way he thought his bye-bye car had gone, hoping he would see it. Hope is strong in dogs and does not die easily or quickly.

A while later he saw a wider road, not as dusty, and he trotted towards it. The dirt smelled different, more like people and cars. Maybe this was where his person was?

The morning's wind died down but that made the air hotter. Ben was panting heavily now, his confusion turning into fright. No matter where he looked, all he could see were patches of trees, lots of brush, and dirt. The landscape around him was bleak, harsh, no people, no other dogs.

He kept moving, hoping there was something ahead. There *had* to be something ahead.

There was. But when he bent his head to sniff it, his whole body recoiled.

It was on the side of the road in a messy clump of dark fur, bones, and blood. Ben thought it had been alive at some point, but it sure wasn't now. He circled it, wondering how it had got there, what had happened for it to be in such condition. Was that a head? Yes, maybe it was, still attached, but barely.

I'm not hungry enough to eat this sad thing.

He walked away but looked over his shoulder.

Am I?

A bend in the road led to a cluster of large rocks, leafy trees, and, thankfully, some shade. Ben loped over to it and sat down, then caught a faint whiff of — could it be? — water! On the other side of a tree was a shallow depression in a rock. It held a small amount of water, with a green color. Normally, the stagnant water would have been shunned, ignored. Not today. Ben didn't care. He lapped all of it up in seconds. The big dog was grateful for every drop.

This was a good place to stay for a while. He found some soft sand out of the hot sun, and collapsed.

When was the last time he'd eaten? It had been last night, his kibble in a bowl on the kitchen floor, with the large bowl of fresh water. He whined at the memory.

Maybe that's not a good thing to think about right now, he scolded himself.

His paws were sore from the road. Licking them brought some relief but it also made him thirsty so he decided not to do that anymore, too.

Can't seem to do anything right, he said to himself. *I was a good boy, wasn't I?*

But, I guess, not anymore.

Night came fast and with it more worries. He heard howling far away. Other dogs? The sounds they made weren't friendly, but taunting and scolding.

The trees were filled with flappings and chitterings. He had heard birds before, he knew what they looked like. Or, thought he did. These birds were much larger and tree branches creaked when the birds flew off.

Something touched one of his legs before slithering off. He trembled, but didn't stand up.

Several times he saw the glowing eyes of other creatures passing him, some stopping to stare before they moved on. Ben wondered what they ate, and if by some chance they had something for him? He was too afraid to ask.

He was also afraid of other questions that crowded his head.

What's going to happen to me? Is tomorrow going to be the same — or worse? I thought I'd always be taken care of. I thought I'd always be loved.

I was wrong.

He finally went to sleep, but a sudden shriek woke him. He stood up, shaking his head. Had he imagined that? No, there was another shriek, close by, filled with pain and death. Ben backed up against the rock, hoping for some protection. He whined, ducked his head.

I better not make eye contact with whatever is out there causing something so much suffering.

The night was telling him he was a stranger here, and not welcome.

CHAPTER FOUR
PLEASE STOP

Ben did not want to open his eyes. The previous day wasn't a dream and he did not want to face that fact. His legs were sore from sleeping on the ground. He felt dirty.

What did I do to deserve this? he asked himself over and over.

He explored the area for some time, hoping there might be more water, maybe even something to eat. But his search produced nothing. Well after noon, with the sun high, he decided it would be best to move on.

His stomach was empty and growled with every step. It was more than a day since he had eaten anything, and he was thirsty again.

He was tempted to leave this road, make his way around the heavy brush, give up the search for food and water.

Just give up.

Then he felt a rumble coming from the road into his paws.

Ben watched a vehicle coming towards him. He lifted his head, wagged his tail. It wasn't *his* car, but another one, much larger. He saw there were two people in it as it slowed down.

Please stop. Please stop. I need help.
Please. Stop.

***

"What's that dog doing in the middle of the road?" Hal asked. He braked the utility truck to slow down.

"I dunno. Nobody lives out here, not for miles," his partner, Becky, answered from the passenger seat. "Pull over."

Becky opened her door to get a better look at the dog.

"Hey, dude, whatcha doing? Pretty hot to be standing in the sun." She checked the truck's reading of outside temperatures. "It's almost ninety-five degrees. Sheesh, all that fur, no wonder you're panting like a tadpole on a river bank."

To her surprise, the dog jumped up enough to put his paws on the running board. "He looks happy to see us," she said, getting down from her seat. "Want some water?"

"Hey, Beck, we shouldn't do that…" Hal started to say but it was too late. Becky grabbed a water bottle and was cupping the liquid in her hand for the dog to slurp up, his tail wagging happily. Seconds later she poured more water, then opened a second bottle for him.

She patted the dog's head, noticing the collar around his neck. "Maybe there are tags," she muttered, twisting the collar around.

"Oh, there's a metal name plate on it. Ben." The dog seemed to smile at the sound of his name. "Ben," she repeated. "Sorry we don't have anything to eat." She patted his head. "We ate our lunch, nothing left."

She looked up and down the road. The nearest ranch was at least ten miles away. The road ended there, turning into narrow trails leading into the mountains.

"We'll take him back to town, maybe drop him off at the shelter, after our shift," she decided, looking up at Hal. "It's on the way to the shop. He's a beautiful dog, somebody's got to be missing him." She opened the club cab door and Ben jumped in, just like he knew he was supposed to, and sat on the seat. "He's sure happy to see us, look at that goofy smile."

Hal grunted. "The office won't like this. Hope he doesn't throw up on the back seat. If he does, you're cleaning it." He was in a bad mood. He was supposed to be Becky's boss, she was only a summer intern, but the girl was stubborn and impetuous. Fortunately, he only had one more week to put up with her, then she'd be back in high school.

They were also running late. It had taken longer to do their job than planned. The utility poles and lines they were supposed to check weren't clearly marked on the map and they had been forced to walk through nettles and scrub oak, and up and down gullies, to get to them.

"Nobody will know," Becky assured him. "We have only two more lines to check. We'll be heading back to town by six o'clock."

***

Ben wasn't thirsty any more. The water had tasted very good. He was still hungry but he hoped the people would take care of that, too.

The inside of the truck was cool and the back seat felt like heaven after last night. He looked out the window as they traveled down the road. The scenery wasn't very interesting, and he was tired. He thought he could lay down for a nap but the truck suddenly stopped and the people got out, leaving a door open. He watched them walk over to a tall piece of wood, talking and pointing.

Maybe he could still take that nap.

His nose shot up. He caught a slight whiff of something. A wonderful odor of meat, and it was being cooked! Yes, that's what it was, all right. He looked back and forth. Where was it coming from?

The two people disappeared behind some trees. Their voices grew fainter.

He jumped down from the truck through the open door. He picked up the direction of the smell much better now. It was a ways off. Should he stay with the truck, wait for the people to come back?

Waiting. That's what he had done all day. Wait wait wait. For what? For who? No, he wasn't going to wait, why should he? Hunger answered that question for him.

Nose to the air, he followed the wonderful smell.

***

Becky and Hal returned to the truck almost an hour later and immediately saw the dog was gone. They walked around the truck, but no Ben.

"Maybe I shouldn't have left the door open," Hal said.

"You didn't want to help him, anyway." Becky tried not to show her disappointment.

Hal started the truck. Becky looked out the window, thinking they'd see Ben trotting down the road. "Maybe he lives around here after all," she whispered.

But, she doubted it.

CHAPTER FIVE
HELLO, BEN. I'M SID

Sid was camped down at the river, only a mile and less than a thirty-minute walk from town. A secluded spot away from any road, difficult to see unless you were paying attention. He liked it that way, didn't want to be around anybody, and certainly not anywhere near one of the homeless camps. Almost every town and city had them now, camps that had done nothing but grow in size and attract bad attention for some years now. Sid wanted no part of that, especially the bad attention.

The trail to his camp was old and overgrown in spots, framed by a cluster of cottonwoods with low-hanging branches. Sid was wary, looking for any signs somebody might have found it. He had learned these many years to be cautious and not too comfortable.

Satisfied his secret was kept, he came into the clearing where his small tent was. As usual, the sound of water lapping against rocks in the river was reassuring. He liked camping by rivers, even though this time of year they were generally low in flow.

He looked up at the sky, clear of clouds, a few jet trails lingering in a fast-approaching sunset. In just a few weeks he'd be hitching rides on a south-trending road before autumn and unpredictable weather set in. While he liked this town, the winters were brutal.

He set his bag down and emptied it. Besides the sack

from the deli, he also had four bottles of water and a can of soda. A small fire pit was nearby. He gathered some sticks and kindling and proceeded to start a flame to cook his dinner. He brought a skillet, a metal plate, and some tableware from the tent. It wasn't long before the pork chops were sizzling in the pan. This would be one of the finest suppers he'd had in some time, and it was all his.

Until he looked up, and through the thick smoke, saw a pair of amber eyes watching him.

***

Ben approached the smoky haze warily. He had never been this hungry before.

That kind of hunger was enough to make any dog mean and angry. But Ben wasn't that kind of dog. He could never be mean. Or angry. So, he did what he always did when he had to wait for something. He inched as close as he dared, sat down, and, on this day, stared into a stranger's dark brown eyes.

***

Sid cleared his throat. "Looks like you've been on the road a while," he said. "Want some of this?" He nodded at the pork chops, now almost done. He stabbed one of them with a fork. "Pretty hot, still."

He shifted his weight to get a closer look at the dog. Big one with golden fur under all that dust. "Are you hurt?

Lost?"

He held out the chop. "You can come closer, I ain't gonna bite you as long as you don't bite me," he chuckled.

***

Ben could not resist any longer. He gently but firmly grabbed the meat between his teeth, then stepped back a few feet. The pork chop was barely chewed, the taste barely savored. All Ben wanted was to get it into his belly as soon as possible, which right now meant seconds.

***

The dog looked at Sid with such obvious gratitude that Sid couldn't help giving him a second pork chop, just as immediately devoured. "Now, I don't mind giving you half my meal," he told the dog, "but I can't give you all of it." He looked about, saw the containers of mac and cheese.

"Might not be the best thing for a dog, I suppose, but then again I suppose there might be an exception now and then." He opened two of the containers, and watched the dog eat, a little slower now, but with determination.

Sid ate the two remaining pork chops and one of the mac and cheese containers while the dog sat and watched.

"How about we go down to the river and get washed up?" Sid suggested. He needed to clean the pan, too.

He started down the path to the water's edge a hundred feet away, then turned back. The dog hadn't followed him.

Maybe he was a wanderer like Sid, ready to hit the road again?

"You coming?" Sid asked.

***

Ben wasn't sure. He knew the man wanted him to follow, but should he? The pull of going back to look for his own person was strong. He looked around, side to side, and behind him. But where exactly was "going back" and how would he get there now? Nothing smelled familiar, nothing looked familiar.

He decided to follow the man to the river.

***

Sid washed the pan and utensils, then sat on the sandy bank to watch the big dog lap at the river's water before wading in. "Bet the cold water feels good on your paws, right?" he asked.

The dog's tail wagged in a lazy manner.

***

Ben's baths were usually in a tub of hot water, but the river was soothing and cool after the long, hot days he had endured. He waded into deeper water and swam a few feet out, happy to be rid of the dust and dirt in his fur.

He returned to the shore and shook himself, sending big

drops of water around him.

***

Sid knew the dog would be shaking off the water, and with his long fur, there would be a **lot** of it in that process. He stood up and moved away from the water's edge before that happened.

Sid saw the dog had a collar. Maybe tags, too. He reached out a hand and made a clicking sound. "Come here, let me take a look at you."

The dog lowered his head, but obeyed and got close enough for Sid to pat his damp head and inspect his collar. No tags, but he saw the metal plate.

"Ben. Your name is Ben. Hello, Ben. I'm Sid.

"I bet you're a good boy, Ben." Sid stared into the dog's big, amber eyes. "Yes, you're a good boy, Ben."

***

Three Magic Words. "Good boy, Ben." He placed a wet paw on the man's leg and was rewarded with a good ear scratching.

For the first time, he saw Sid's eyes had a deep, sad kindness that, on this day, mirrored his own.

CHAPTER SIX
DR. SHEILA, D.V.M.

Two hundred miles away, in a large town, a meeting was about to begin. The subject was a growing and vexing problem in their community: *Homelessness, Vagrancy, and Vandalism.*

The room was already hot and stuffy. Some people had found early seats, others stood around talking to each other in low tones.

Veterinarians Dr. Sheila and her husband Dr. Jim had arrived early and were sitting near the front. "There are more than a hundred people here. I wonder who are friends of the homeless, and who are foes," she whispered to him.

"I'm guessing we're about to find out," he whispered back.

At the front of the large room sat the assortment of city council members and their staff. She recognized at least three lawyers in the audience, which set a less-than-positive tone.

Television cameras were set up and reporters with microphones or notepads mingled with the crowd, asking questions, getting comments.

Days before the meeting, representatives of several organizations and groups had signed up to speak, Dr. Sheila among them. There would also be time for public comments. Before entering the town hall, agendas had been handed out. At the top of the paper was the admonishment:

Violence and foul language will not be tolerated! Respect will be shown to each speaker, do not interrupt. Handing out flyers strictly prohibited!

Dr. Jim held a large stack of folders on his lap. "Sure hope we have enough for all of the council members and their staff."

"If we need more, I'll tell them we'll deliver more in the morning," she nodded. "I just hope they're not considered 'flyers' and we get arrested for handing them out."

He snorted a chuckle.

She wasn't used to making public presentations, especially for something this important. She was dressed in a smart blue suit with a short jacket; her brown hair was combed away from an oval face. She had light green eyes and a wide smile. Now in her 40s, she was an accomplished veterinarian, and with her husband owned one of the more successful veterinary hospitals in the area.

The first four people took their turns to speak, introducing themselves as representatives of this or that organization. Some came prepared with facts:

- "More than 50 homeless people camp out at Sparrow Park any given night."
- "There are dozens of homeless tents and makeshift lean-tos all along our river banks."
- "Cops show up every few weeks to tear them down, cart the mess away, but a few days later it's all back, maybe even worse than ever."

To exaggerations:

- "All of them are drunk or on drugs, every single one of them."
- "They're criminals, can't trust them, they'll steal anything, then sell it on the streets and head to the nearest liquor store or drug dealer."

To a few emotional pleas for compassion:

- "They are people just like us, down on their luck, they need help."
- "Homelessness isn't against the law."

Dr. Sheila noticed this last one was met with head shaking and eye rolling from many in the audience.

One of the area's leading businessmen got up to speak. He owned a large sports shop on Main Street.

"We have tried lots of different approaches." He sounded sympathetic. "We have public restrooms which were being vandalized almost every night. So, we piped in loud, and I might say obnoxious music, to discourage their usage. Finally, we just ended up locking the restroom's doors unless we have a special event during the day.

"Next we thought about spraying the homeless with fire hoses when they fell asleep on our sidewalks, in breezeways, or alleys. Now, some of you might think that would be a fine thing during the summer," he paused to look around him, appreciating the snickers of laughter, "but in the winter that might be considered cruel. So that plan was nixed.

"I realize, as do many of my fellow Main Street store

owners, that some of you might not know what we're dealing with. These people —"

And with that one phrase, "*these people*," Dr. Sheila braced herself, realizing this man was anything but sympathetic.

"— come into our stores looking to use restrooms or bum a cup of coffee. They intimidate customers. Things disappear. Folks, you've already heard that shoplifting is a real problem, and it's almost impossible to keep track of. We get no help from law enforcement in our town, since we don't know who's breaking the law.

"What can we do? Some of us are considering buying low-impact pellet guns and shoot them before they come in, just as they open the door." There was a ripple of chuckles in the audience but the officials at the front, especially the lawyers, suddenly sat up with attention.

"Now, we understand that seems extreme," he held up his hands and plowed on, "but with the lack of law enforcement or any kind of help, what can we do? The pellet guns won't cause any permanent harm, it's just to let them know they're not wanted on Main Street. We'll take a training course, become real marksmen. That's a plan, and we think it's a good one." With that he sat down, with a shocking number of people applauding him.

A woman shouted out, "Just like the wild, wild west!" She was gaveled to silence but not before the audience erupted in laughter.

"Until somebody shoots out an eye," Dr. Jim muttered to his wife. He glanced down at the agenda. "You're up next. Tough act to follow."

She shot him a "thanks for nothing" glance, took the folders, then made her way to the podium.

She introduced herself as the owner, with her husband, of Kaufman Veterinary Hospital. "Looking around, I see some of our clients here." She smiled, hoping she was in friendly territory, but not entirely certain. There were a few nods in the audience. She adjusted her glasses, swept some strands of hair back, then continued.

"I am speaking for many of the veterinarians in town. Like many of you, we have also seen the growing impact of the homeless in our community. I admit," she looked to the previous speaker, and nodded to him, "I did not know the impact this is having on our local businesses, and I also admit I do not have a solution. I am here to talk about another concern: Namely, the fact that many of them now have dogs and puppies, animals that are neither neutered nor vaccinated."

There were murmurs of agreement. One councilwoman leaned into her microphone. "They're with their dogs on almost every street corner. We're assuming that they're being used to evoke sympathy from passing motorists. Get more money."

"Shameful, using animals this way," a man in the audience loudly agreed.

Dr. Sheila nodded. "I agree, it is shameful, but the reality is people have used animals to entertain us, make money for us, for centuries, sometimes in awful ways. Circuses, carnivals, road side attractions. Dog fighting is still acceptable in some areas." She held up her hands. "I'm not here to defend or criticize. Sure, the dogs are used by the homeless to pull at our heartstrings. But at the same time, these dogs might do what they do in our homes. Give us love and warmth and I'm guessing for some of the homeless it could be the only love and warmth they receive.

"What I am here to do is ask our city and county leaders to recognize the concerns we have as veterinarians. Besides indiscriminate and uncontrollable breeding, there is also a genuine risk that some dogs have highly communicable diseases, such as distemper, kennel cough, and of course rabies, which is chief among our worries. The camps down by the river are not the safest environments. Our own pets might be at risk."

That got everybody's attention.

"The local veterinarian's organization has been awarded a grant, twenty-five thousand dollars, to hold clinics this year. Spaying, neutering, and vaccinations, free of charge. We will donate our time and expertise."

She paused, organizing her notes. "This has been done with quite a bit of success in several other communities. A veterinary hospital in Denver will loan us their mobile surgical trailer.

"It's a matching grant. We are asking the city to please consider our request to give us the other twenty-five thousand dollars. This money will go a long way to help this problem, and protect all of our pets. We would like to start next month. I have packets with all of the information about the grant and our plans." She handed the bundle to a staff member. "And of course, if you have any questions, I'll be happy to answer." She looked up. "There is a lot of support for this and we hope you'll support it, too.''

A council member asked, "This is for one year, what about next year, or the year after?"

"Fair question," Dr. Sheila said. "We can apply for and get other grants. We will be completely transparent with all of the results and document everything. We feel very strongly that this will get a lot of attention." She turned to look at the audience. "Your town's veterinarians are really eager to make this work, it's that important."

The businessman who wanted to shoot people with pellet guns raised his hand and stood up. "I imagine you're taking donations," he reached for his back pocket and pulled out his wallet. "Here." He handed five crisp twenty-dollar bills to a surprised Dr. Sheila. "Let me know if you need more help."

Another surprise: A motion was made, seconded, and carried. The veterinarians would get their money. Finally, somebody had an idea. Not for the homeless but for their dogs.

A staff member told her to work with area agencies. "I'm sure our social services department can give you lots of information," he said. "We'll have somebody contact you."

When Dr. Sheila turned to walk back down the aisle to her seat, she was met with a mass of cameras and microphones. Reporters followed her down the aisle and out the door.

CHAPTER SEVEN
POSTERS

Ben sat down in the dirt next to the opening where Sid had disappeared. He was told it was called a "tent" and that's where Sid slept.

He wasn't invited inside, and he wasn't the kind of dog who would intrude or nose his way in.

He glanced around. It was dark but his sharp eyes picked up the nearby brush, shrubs, and trees. His ears picked up the rustling of leaves. Small animals, much smaller than he was, moved about.

Plop, plop. Something jumped into the river, making Ben's ears twitch. He wasn't curious about what had made that sound, and his senses did not pick up anything that he should be concerned about, either. His belly was full, the river was nearby. He felt much safer than he had in the previous night.

He found a soft patch of grass, so he curled up and was soon asleep.

***

Sid stretched himself awake the next morning. The sun was dappled inside his tent, the blues and greens of the fabric blending together. This was his favorite part of the day, laying in the warmth of his sleeping bag. There might be worries and troubles outside the tent, but for these few minutes they would leave Sid alone.

He reached over to unzip the flap leading to the outside. He was surprised to see the big dog lying in some grass a few feet away, but was sort of glad. Then he was surprised he was glad. The dog raised his head in a sleepy kind of way, gave his goofy smile, and wagged his tail in greeting.

"You still here?" Sid asked, feeling silly asking the question. The night before, after dark, Sid had climbed into his small tent but left Ben outside. He thought perhaps the dog would take off, maybe find his way home. But no, here he was, a mess of gold fur. looking at him.

Why did he feel guilty for leaving the dog to sleep outside?

"Expecting breakfast?" Sid asked, and crawled out. He stood up, yawned, and rolled his shoulders. "Arthritis," he told Ben. "You don't wanna grow old, dude."

He felt the dog's eyes on him as he slipped on his jeans from yesterday, then took out a clean t-shirt from the backpack propped up against the tent.

The river's water was cold and he quickly washed up, scrubbing his face. Sid could never grow a decent beard and had long since stopped trying, which was fine. Long, unkempt facial hair was not looked on with favor by the folks he encountered in a town or on the road. His black hair was thick, however, and he had to take scissors to it quite often. He occasionally indulged in free haircuts when and where they might be offered.

"Only cold bagels for breakfast," Sid told Ben, shaking off his wet hands. "Probably not good for you, but you look

OK after eating the mac and cheese last night, so…" he let the thought trail away and handed Ben the roll.

***

Ben chewed on the bagel, not particularly liking it but wanting to be polite. He didn't think it would be a good idea to reject it.

He drank more water from the river, then raised his leg a time or two on some trees.

He was still worried. What was going to happen this day? Would this person abandon him, too? Would there be more food? He'd never had to ask these questions before but the last two days haunted him, filling him with doubts.

***

Sid tidied up his camp site, putting containers in a paper bag. He'd toss them in a trash bin in town. A lid had drifted off into some nearby brush and he bent down to pick it up.

"Hey, look what I found!" He turned to the dog, an old tennis ball, faded from sun and years, in his hand. "I bet you'd like to play, wouldn't you?" It was a logical question, after all. Here was a dog. Here was a ball.

The dog tilted his head and began to walk away.

"Wait, go catch!" He threw the ball as far as he could. It landed with a pathetic bounce in the dirt.

Did that dog just shrug? Sid asked himself.

***

Are you nuts? Ben thought. *You really think I'm going to fall for that again? You must think I'm the stupidest dog in the world. No way am I going to chase after that ratty old thing. I know what you're trying to do.*

He shook his head, trying to dislodge the memory of watching the bye-bye car disappear down that dirt road leaving him alone, thirsty, and hungry.

Ben stood up, walked away with a flick of his tail but turned back to stare at Sid.

Maybe I was wrong about you. I'm very disappointed.

***

Sid watched Ben walk away. "Huh," he said out loud. If he hadn't known better the dog looked at him as though he was disappointed. Dogs can't be disappointed, can they?

"Wait, it's OK," he trotted after Ben. "Didn't mean anything by it. You're just not a fetchin' kind of dog. I get it. I promise, I'll never do that again!"

He bent down to pat Ben's head, ruffling up the fur. "Pretty ratty ol' ball anyway, you wouldn't want that in your mouth. Here. Want a cookie?"

***

Ben was mollified, but only slightly. He watched Sid grab a canvas bag and motioned for him to come. Ben got up and reluctantly followed.

***

Sid retraced his steps from the day before back to the road. He didn't have to look behind him to know that Ben followed him, the dog inspecting and sniffing every bush and tree and making a great deal of noise doing it.

It was still early, before nine o'clock. Sid wasn't looking for any traffic on the road. He was looking for utility poles, not because he was interested in utility poles, but what they often sported: The myriad of posters with sad and pleadings messages about lost and found dogs and cats.

Occasionally human faces were on the posters. Missing children, almost always teenagers, boys and girls smiling in happier times but now causing great worry for parents.

You could learn a lot from a town's utility poles. Over the years they had become bulletin boards, replacing town newspaper's "Lost and Found" sections, even replacing the newspapers themselves.

Closer to town the posters were more prolific, stapled or nailed on both sides. Sid hadn't spotted any for a lost or missing Golden Retriever or any large dog. More than half were for lost cats, and the rest for smaller dogs. Some might be found, most wouldn't. He suspected coyotes or mountain lions, bulking up for the coming winter months, were the likely reason.

He stopped for a minute to take a drink from his water bottle, then offered some to Ben in a plastic bowl from his pack.

"Recognize anything, dude?" Sid asked. By now there were a few cars and trucks on the road, but none had slowed down. Ben turned around, then turned around again, looking up and down the road.

Sid wasn't sure what to think.

"Somebody has to be missing you," he muttered, shaking his head. "You're a first-rate dog, pure bred. Cost a lot of money, I'm betting." He reached down to scratch behind Ben's ears. He stood straight again, and, mimicking the dog, looked up and down the road.

"I don't get it."

***

Ben didn't get it, either. He didn't know what he was supposed to do.

Can dogs forget what has happened to them in the past? Some can, maybe some can't. Or maybe it's somewhere in between. *That would be me.* Yes, he decided, he was somewhere in between. A half-forgettin' half-rememberin' kind of dog. And he was fast forgettin' what his bye-bye car had even looked like.

With that, he nudged Sid's hand. *"I'm all right. Now, let's go wherever you decide we're going to go.*

"By the way, I forgive you for trying to trick me with that ball. But, please don't do it again."

***

They were close to the outskirts of the town's shopping district. Some stores were open, some not this early in the morning. Music was coming from somewhere and Sid paused for a few minutes. A woman singing, one of the new songs people were listening to. When he was younger, his parents would describe it as a "toe tapper."

Music was one of the things Sid missed. At one time he had a portable CD player but it broke and he hadn't replaced it. Maybe he would in a month or two, buy a couple of new CDs. Maybe one with this song on it.

They passed other stores. Most weren't open yet, it was too early, and the parking lots were empty. Sid paused at the door of a business supply store. A sign covered most of the glass:

No vagrants or dogs allowed!
Keep out!

He had seen these signs before but never paid them no mind, the warning only half-pertaining to him. Looking down at Ben, now all of it did.

Sid headed to the organic grocery story on the other end of town.

Tess, the owner, was friendly. Sometimes she had a small job for him to do, sweeping the sidewalk or fixing cabinet hardware. Her doors did not have any kind of "Keep out" signs on them.

He liked the small store. It had an old-fashioned appeal, walls covered with gleaming wood shelves and drawers. The odors of decades of spices and fresh produce filled the air.

Tess looked up from the long counter. She was in her late 30s, tall, with a mop of reddish blonde hair. She had a long apron over her jeans and checkered shirt.

"Sid, come on in! Oh — you have a friend!" She started to reach down to pet him, then withdrew her hand. "Is he friendly?"

"So far. He's a big tub of drool and that tail will sweep your floor in no time," Sid chuckled.

"He *is* big, seventy pounds, I'm guessing," she agreed, patting his head, then gently opened his mouth. Tess seemed to know a little about dogs "Two years old, maybe? How'd you come by him?"

"Just showed up at my camp. Real hungry like he hadn't eaten in days. His name is Ben, says on the collar, but no tags. Somebody might be looking for him."

She clicked her tongue and shook her head. "Not neutered. No tags. That's always a bad sign. You gotta know that." She straightened back up. "Usually means he's been dumped."

"Really? That seems..." Sid struggled for the word. "Needless."

"You just never know. This is a tourist town and folks travel with their dogs but it gets to be a chore or their dogs get tired of it and take off. Maybe they stopped at a gas station or motel and the dog escapes or just wanders away. Usually, the owners do a good job looking, stay an extra day or two, but sometimes they don't, have to hit the road, get back home or wherever they're going. They leave their name and number at the city animal shelter, but," she shrugged, "the shelter can only do so much. Maybe their dog will turn up, maybe not. It's sad."

Sid looked down at Ben. "I suppose I can take him to the shelter, like you said, they might have some word on him?"

Tess was skeptical. "If you do, and nobody claims him, or nobody adopts him, they have a pretty strict three-day rule."

He knew what that meant. "They'll put him down."

She nodded. "I'll call them later this morning, ask if somebody has reported a lost golden. I'll just say a friend found one."

She pulled her phone from her pocket. "There's a lost and found site on the web, really active, lots of people on it." A few clicks and she shook her head. "Don't see anything."

Sid held back a sigh. This wasn't what he expected, not at all. He was only trying to help the dog, but it was getting, well, complicated.

"I have some things for you." Tess went around a counter and began to pull out a variety of items from a large cooler. Six pre-wrapped sandwiches and several apples were placed in a paper sack. She produced a bag of chips at another counter, as well as a few energy bars. All went into the same sack.

Finally, a ten-pound bag of dog food came from a shelf. "This won't last him long," she laughed and nodded at Ben, "but I don't want to give you too much to carry. Oh, and our town has a strict leash law, don't want to get stopped by the cops just because of that. Here's a leash for Ben." She snapped it on his collar.

Sid held up his hand and shook his head. "All of this. Too generous."

"You're a good man, Sid, you take it all." She wouldn't hear any more of his protests and ushered him out the door, making sure he had a firm grip on the sack. "Come back tomorrow, I'll hear from the shelter by then and maybe see something on that lost and found website."

CHAPTER EIGHT
THE TOUR

The front page of the morning newspaper was devoted to the city's homeless meeting, with a tongue-in-cheek headline:

VETERINARIANS TO THE RESCUE
PLAN TO "FIX" THE HOMELESS PROBLEM

Dogs pose risk to community, local vet tells city.
Mobile clinic to vaccinate, spay, neuter

"The photographer got a good picture of you." Dr. Jim folded the newspaper and slipped it across the table. He stood up and stretched.

He was a tall man with thinning hair, slightly older than his wife. They were in her office. Both were dressed for their day, casual slacks and cotton shirts with the hospital's logo over a front pocket. The door was open and they could hear the receptionist greeting clients.

Dr. Sheila shook her head. "This isn't exactly what I had in mind. I don't want to be the face of this. And we're not 'fixing' anything."

"The publicity will help. It's a positive story. Unlike some we've seen about homeless people."

Many articles and TV news stories concentrated on substance abuse, vandalism, and unwanted homeless camps.

Efforts by law enforcement to roust them out of town were also great fodder for their articles.

"I'll take over your cases for you while you meet with the social worker," Dr. Jim said.

The city staff member from last night's meeting had kept his promise. Just after eight o'clock that morning a social services employee called to set up a meeting with Dr. Sheila.

She grabbed her bag, making sure her cell phone was in it. "Thanks. I have two cats coming in for spays, and a teeth cleaning for Mugsy, the Schnauzer. I'm sure I'll be back by noon for our afternoon appointments. I'm hoping my learning curve gets flattened after today and we'll have all we need to know."

***

Connie sat down in a chair across from Sheriff Stewart's desk.

He looked up and smiled, noticing her khaki pants and short-sleeved shirt. "You're dressed pretty casual for a work day."

"I have to babysit that veterinarian who was at last night's meeting. Show her around, give her the tour."

"Another do-gooder out to save the world, right?"

"Probably. But maybe it's a good idea to get those dogs taken care of." Connie was ready to give the project the benefit of the doubt, but part of her agreed with the sheriff. As the town's homeless coordinator, she had seen many "do-gooders" come and go — mostly go.

"I'll take her down to the smaller camp by the gravel pit."

Sheriff Stewart barked a laugh. He was a short, stocky man. His hair was gray and he was two years from retirement. "Coward. Take her to the big one, let her see what's really going on. Speaking of which," he handed Connie a folder. "We're cleaning it up next week."

She frowned, glancing at the pages. "Next week? You're not giving us a lot of notice."

"I'm sorry about that. But I've got two guys out the end of this month for training, and then there's hunting season. Lots of requests for vacation, you know how it is in the autumn." He paused and looked out the window to avoid making eye contact with Connie. "If we're going to do this, it's got to be next week. This is top secret, got it? The public and certainly the press don't know about this, and we're going to keep it that way."

Connie read out loud from the folder she had just been given. "Ten officers will arrive early before six o'clock to escort the inhabitants who can leave with whatever they can carry. Bulldozers and trucks will follow to remove tents, shelters, bags, trash, and whatever else is left. The area will be scraped clean and fencing erected to ensure the camp is not re-established.

"There are more than two hundred men in those camps, a few women," Connie looked up from the report. "They'll swarm the streets, people will complain, they'll have nowhere to go."

"That's why we're letting social services know. You're their homeless coordinator, right? So, coordinate. Whatever housing you can find. We'll have a bus to take them to wherever you say."

Connie shook her head. "This is a joke, right?"

He shrugged again. "Like I said, sorry."

She rubbed her temple. "Now I got another headache." She stood up to leave. "We've got to talk about what's happening in other towns. Those vigilantes calling themselves 'Rippers.'"

"Stupid kids talking big on the Internet. Bragging. Gonna raid homeless camps, cut up their tents, scare them away. They think everything's a video game," the sheriff said. "So far a couple of times in big cities."

"Yeah, so far, but it's just a matter of time before somebody gets hurt," Connie said.

"Not in our town. People are concerned about the homeless, but they're not ready to take the law into their own hands."

"Except for the store owner who wants to shoot them…" she began.

"With a pellet gun, not a real one." He waved her out of his office. "Let's not take it that seriously. No reason to scare these folks, OK?"

***

Dr. Sheila entered the police station lobby and saw an older woman with friendly eyes. "Are you Connie?"

They shook hands. "My department head asked me to help you," Connie said, "answer any questions you have, introduce you to some people. What got you interested in the homeless issue?"

"Their dogs, seeing them on street corners, in city parks, or walking with their owners on the side of the road. But their dogs get hit by cars or are injured in some other way, needing emergency treatment. Dogs that are still puppies but having puppies. Or are very sick but..." she paused, "too sick for us to do anything. There's no money to treat them, of course, and that puts veterinarians in a terrible situation.

"We reached out to veterinarians in other towns last year and found they are having the same problems. It was time to be pro-active, at least as much as we can. Spaying, neutering, routine vaccinations. A fund to treat these animals when there's an emergency. But," Dr. Sheila admitted, "that's a long-term goal."

Connie nodded. "You gave the city a lot to think about last night."

"How long have you been with social services?"

"Almost twenty years now, but I was assigned to the needs of the homeless five years ago. It's been..." she bit her lower lip, "an interesting assignment."

***

Connie's car, an SUV provided by the county with the social services logo on each door, was parked in the hot sun but air conditioning soon made the interior comfortable. Connie steered the car into traffic.

"Do homeless people get arrested a lot?" Dr. Sheila

asked.

Connie shook her head. "No, most of the contacts police make are welfare checks, maybe they heard of somebody who's been hurt, somebody who might need help with a medical emergency, getting to a clinic or a doctor. Last week there were two men in a verbal disagreement but calmed down quickly when officers arrived."

She looked over at Dr. Sheila. "If they arrested all of the homeless for whatever minor incident, our local jail would be full for weeks, with no room for serious criminals.

"And we would have no idea what we'd do with their dogs. Our animal shelters are always full as it is. That's given us a new challenge for this population."

Dr. Sheila nodded. "'This population'...that's a term I hear a lot. Doesn't it kind of dehumanize them?"

"Sure," Connie shrugged, pulling into the large parking lot of a church. "Dehumanizing them is acceptable. Look, we've hated them, feared them, cussed at them, thrown things at them, but none of that's worked. The problem is," Connie shook her head, "we don't know what's going to work...for this population.

"Anyway, we're here, our first stop. There's somebody you should meet. He's on the front lines fighting the good fight."

***

Connie led the way to the church's side area. "Every Tuesday this church has a give-away for people in need.

Anybody can come and look for items they might find useful."

"Even if they're not homeless?"

Connie chuckled. "They don't ask for proof of homelessness. They figure if somebody's going to show up here, they need it, and that's all that's important."

There were several tables piled high with clothes and shoes. Other tables had dishes, cookware, and other household items, all used, but looking to be in good condition.

"This is the only church that has these donation tables every week," Connie explained. "A few others do it monthly or perhaps three or four times a year. Especially in the winter."

They watched as several men and a couple of women picked through the mounds, a few chatting with each other.

Some had dogs, most of them small, less than twenty pounds, only a few were slightly larger. That made sense, Dr. Sheila thought. Feeding big dogs would be expensive.

The dogs were well behaved, some barked a little, tails wagging in a friendly fashion.

"Most of the dogs are on leashes," she observed.

Connie nodded. "Homeless people will obey *those* laws since a dog off-leash is easy to spot by law enforcement. They'll always avoid any kind of attention."

She waved to a man who sauntered over. He was balding, dressed in shorts and a casual shirt. He looked to be about sixty years old. His eyes crinkled into a smile.

Connie introduced him to Dr. Sheila. "This is Pastor

Larry. He's been working with homeless people for many years." She smiled at him. "I promised Dr. Sheila some preachy stuff."

He laughed and shook the veterinarian's hand. "I'll try to oblige. I saw your picture in this morning's paper," he said. "You have a good idea, reaching out to the homeless to help their dogs."

"I have to be honest, a lot of what I know is what I've read online or in the media," Dr. Sheila confessed. "One question I have is pretty simple. Who are these people, where do they come from?"

"Years ago, homeless people were called transients, tramps, or hobos," he answered. "Men hitchhiking, riding the rails. Maybe looking for a handout but mostly looking for some work before they headed south in the winter, north in the summer. But now?"

His next words were shocking.

"Most of the people you see here and on the street corners? They're from these parts, our town or nearby. Maybe they were your neighbors."

She blinked. "How is that possible?"

"A lot of people, men and women of all ages, are just a month away from being homeless," he said. "You lose your job, you have an unexpected bill. Health problems. Divorce is a big reason why many lose their homes, and everything they've ever owned. Kids, teenagers, get kicked out. That happens, too.

"People are afraid of homeless people. But a lot of those same people are afraid of becoming homeless themselves.

There's real fear out there. On all sides."

Dr. Sheila pursed her lips. "Our winters get really bad, lots of snow, freezing temperatures. But they only have tents, lean-tos. How do they get by?"

"In truth, some don't." He shook his head. "It's a terrible struggle. Every year a few are found in bad health from the cold. Some don't make it. They die. But remember our summers get horribly hot. That heat wave last month? Terrible suffering, heat stroke, dehydration. We have three homeless shelters, but they fill up very fast by afternoon, and turn away dozens."

Connie turned to face Dr. Sheila. "One of those shelters is near your veterinary hospital," she said. "We haven't had a chance to inspect it, yet, so I don't know too much about how it's run."

Dr. Sheila nodded. "It opened about a year ago, across from our parking lot."

Pastor Larry continued. "Besides the shelters, there are several organizations that provide rooms or apartments. Women with children get the priority, we try very hard to reach out to them as soon as we see them on the streets."

He paused, nodding to Connie. "We don't get all of them, but we try. Anything we can, wherever we can."

They watched as a few more men and women picked through the tables, which by now were almost cleared off.

Connie nodded to a figure near the end. "Who's that, is he new?"

"That's Ryan, showed up here a few weeks ago. Kind of shy. When I introduced myself, he was friendly enough but didn't say a lot about where he'd come from. He says he's eighteen, but..." Pastor Larry looked knowingly at Connie, "for my money he's a *lot* younger. I know he's picked up an odd job or two, but I'm not sure he has any ID on him. A teenager like that is fragile, vulnerable." He took a deep breath. "A lot of bad things happen to kids on the streets."

A little dog quickly darted out from under a table to sniff at the grass. The boy whistled and the dog obediently returned to his side and was scooped up.

"Terrier. We need to get that young man a leash for his dog," Dr. Sheila muttered.

"A customer for your vet services," Pastor Larry laughed.

"And he's also mine," Connie added when they saw an inhaler suddenly appear from a pocket and the boy drew in a large breath. "Asthma. I'll make sure he gets refills on that prescription."

"You do that, too?" Dr. Sheila asked.

Connie and Pastor Larry exchanged another look, and she repeated his words:

"Anything we can, wherever we can."

CHAPTER NINE
CREATURE COMFORTS

Ryan saw the three adults pointing his way while he picked through the clothes on the table. He wasn't stupid, he knew they were talking about him, and it scared him.

Fear, stress, uncertainty, always a problem with his asthma. He drew his inhaler from a pocket and took a deep draw.

He grabbed a couple of t-shirts from the table, stuffed them in a small sack, then called to his little dog. "Come on, Classy, we're outta here." He decided they wouldn't be coming back to this church anytime soon. He was sure they were on to him.

Classy scampered after her owner, just inches behind his feet. She had been with Ryan since she was a puppy, going on ten years now, loyal to Ryan and always looking for ways to please him.

A block away he slowed down, away from the church, away from the people looking at him. He did not want any attention, nor questions about who he was or where he came from. He was only sixteen years old and he knew people would wonder why wasn't he home, why wasn't he in school?

The answers were simple: he didn't have a home and nobody cared about him. He hated school anyway, always had problems keeping up with the other kids.

He was small for his age, not athletic at all, and, of course, there was the asthma. He had to deal with that all the time, and it made him angry when people said he was faking it, not really sick. Asthma isn't a real disease anyway, he'd been told. People like his stepdad, always picking on him.

A cool breeze ruffled his long dark brown hair. He took out a portable music player and his headphones. A few seconds later he was walking to the beat of his favorite rock band.

In an alley-way he saw some cardboard boxes sticking out of a dumpster. He grabbed one, tore it in half and from his pack drew out a black marker.

GOOD WORKER. MOW LAWNS. TRIM. PULL WEEDS. CHEAP. $5 AN HOUR. COLD WATER APPRECIATED.

It was going to be another hot day, standing on a street corner with that sign. The fact he was young helped a little, and Classy helped, too. Like most terriers, she was cute.

But the sign also said he'd work cheap and surprisingly that was a different "pitch" than most of the street corner panhandlers.

He had been picked up several times, taken to nice homes to mow their lawns. He liked that kind of work, maybe because he couldn't do much else, but at least he might get ten or fifteen dollars that day and almost always some cold water, tea, or sodas. The owner might give Classy a treat or two. She could lay in the shade of a big tree, and take a long nap while he worked. Nothing wrong with that.

Sign made, he picked a street corner where people would be coming and going to nearby subdivisions. With Classy at his side, he waited.

He watched as the county SUV carrying the two women from the church passed by, wondering where they might be going.

***

Connie drove over the bridge, then took a rough dirt road with deep ruts. She obviously knew it well, steering around larger holes, careful not to get her car stuck in deep dirt.

"The larger camps are down by the river, south of downtown," she explained. "I figured I'd show you one of the smaller camps, with not many people." She pointed to a large pond. "There are some abandoned gravel pits over there, where they can get water and swim."

"And mosquitos, carrying heartworm to the dogs," Dr. Sheila observed. "Does the county spray these ponds?"

"I don't know," was Connie's response.

Another possible problem to solve.

The area was lined with cattails, cottonwoods, and many elms, shade against the sun but their leaves dry from the hot summer.

A sharp bend in the road revealed a few tents. They were a hodge-podge of faded colors and quality. A couple of them looked new, some were little better than rags providing scant shelter against whatever any weather might attack them. A hundred feet further, large canvas canopies stretched from tree to tree.

Near the center of a clearing was a small, very ancient, and very rusty, van sitting on its axles. If it had ever moved, it was years, maybe decades ago. All of the van's glass windows were long gone and covered with sheets of canvas or other materials, as was the side door.

Propped up against a tree was a newer bicycle hitched to a two-wheeled bike hauler for carrying small items.

A tall, older man now came out of that door, holding a can of soda.

Connie stopped her SUV. "Generally, I bring a few boxes of food and bottled water," she explained, getting out and opening up the back. "It helps them to know I'm a friendly, not an enemy." She smiled wanly.

"Hi, Rex, how's it going?" she called over to the man. "Did you get a new bike?"

"Yeah, a shop was giving away some used ones. But this one looks pretty new. Need some help?" he asked as Connie pulled out a sack of groceries.

Rex had a long, white beard and even longer white hair. He wore a pair of faded jeans and a short-sleeved button shirt. Both looked clean. Dr. Sheila noticed his hands were also clean, his finger nails short and well-kept.

Connie introduced Dr. Sheila and briefly told him the

plans for the mobile veterinary clinic. He smiled and thought for a moment, then said, "That will be a good thing. Not everybody will think so, but most will."

A small boxer mix came bounding out of the van. "This is Brutus," was the introduction. Brutus was a stout, handsome dog, brindle-colored with a snub-nosed snout. "He's friendly, sweet as a lollypop."

Dr. Sheila bent down to pet him; she saw he had been neutered. Rex somehow knew what she was thinking.

"Me and my wife got him years ago from one of the shelters. Already fixed and vax'd. Uhm, ex-wife, I should say. I was a mechanic, pretty good one, then I had an accident, got hurt. Medical bills did us in. She got the house, I got Brutus." The look on his face conveyed he thought he'd gotten the better deal. He didn't have to finish his story, the accident and divorce were the reasons he now lived in a run-down van.

Rex and Dr. Sheila helped Connie with several more bags and boxes, following her to an old picnic table, which was little better than splintered wood. The surface was soon covered with dozens of canned vegetables, soups, bread, cereal, oatmeal, and cookies.

Rex carried three large bags of dog food to the shade of a nearby tree then returned to help unload clusters of bottled water.

That task done, Dr. Sheila looked about. "Where is everybody?"

"Most of them are on the streets, they leave early to catch morning commuters, panhandling for money, before it gets too hot," Rex explained. "Generally, one of us stays here most of the day, keeping an eye on things. We trade off. Make sure nothing disappears."

Sheila tilted her head. "You mean...people will steal from you? I mean, no offense, but," she looked around, "...what is there to steal?"

Rex smiled. "No offense taken, but if you have nothing, then anything somebody else has can look pretty appealing."

"Especially cell phones," Connie added.

Dr. Sheila frowned. "You have cell phones?" she asked Rex.

"A lot of us do. You have to qualify but the government gives them to us. But if you lose one, or lose it too many times, they'll disqualify you. So..." he shrugged, "people steal them."

She shook her head. "The homeless stealing from the homeless," she murmured.

Rex put his hands in his pockets. "Thieves live in homeless camps. They also live in million-dollar houses."

That shocked her, and she had nothing to say.

Rex continued. "We also have problems getting the phones charged. Our camps don't have electricity, as I'm sure you've noticed," he smiled. "We look for places to plug them in wherever we can."

Dr. Sheila shook her head. Her "learning curve" for homeless issues was getting curvier.

She asked how many people in this camp had dogs. He thought for a moment before answering.

"Right now, about a dozen, but that number changes."

He hesitated. "Dogs come and go, they run off, or maybe get picked up because they don't have tags." He shook his head. "To get tags, you gotta have an address." His hands swept around the clearing. "No address here."

Dr. Sheila made another mental note. Yet another possible problem to solve.

The two women got ready to leave.

Rex reached down to scratch Brutus' head. "A lot of us, well, we love our dogs. People think we don't take care of them, but we do our best. I also know people think we use them, too, to get more money begging on the streets. But look at it this way. People without dogs usually get as much as the ones who do. So, really, what kind of advantage do they give us? Except the advantage of having something to keep us going. And," he smiled, "creature comforts."

They waved good bye and Connie steered her SUV back the way they'd come.

"A tough life," Dr. Sheila said. Seeing this camp, and talking to Rex, had given her a tough swallow of these very real problems.

Connie nodded. "Some have chosen it for themselves because they don't have any family or good friends. Sometimes I think we'll always have a lot of homeless people. Too many. I try not to judge, keep an open mind." She took a deep breath. "But now, we might have a new problem.

"I didn't want to say anything to Rex, didn't want to alarm him. And there's no real indication it'll happen here, in our town. But other cities are hearing more and more about..." she hesitated. "Rippers."

Dr. Sheila swung her head sharply around. "Rippers? What are Rippers?"

"Not what," Connie answered. "Who."

CHAPTER TEN
NIGHTMARES

Ben watched Sid open the sack of dog food. The smell was familiar but not particularly enticing. He had really liked last night's supper and hoped there would be the same, but obviously not. At least he didn't have to eat the hard piece of tasteless whatever that was from this morning.

A paper plate was pushed his way with a good portion of the hard kibble. Ben wagged his tail, letting Sid know it was appreciated.

***

"Probably not what you're expecting," Sid chuckled. "Not as good as those pork chops, but hey, moochers can't be choosers. And you, my friend, are a moocher."

He watched the dog eat for a few seconds then pulled out a sandwich with a bag of chips and sat down. He rested his back against a fallen log, watching the river.

As often as he could, and wherever he was, Sid just liked to sit at his campsite, maybe read a local newspaper or a book he'd found somewhere. People threw books away, which astonished him, but he was in no position to lecture anybody and he appreciated the cast-offs.

He drew out a book from his sack, it was in fine shape. He wondered if anybody had ever read it. A western, which he liked, a story from a century ago. He would have a few more hours of daylight to read before darkness set in. Grabbing another sandwich, he began to flick through the pages.

***

Ben went down to the river for a drink. His lapping was noisy. He sat for a while, watching the water. A few ducks floated by, unconcerned that the dog was watching them.

He yawned. His belly was full and for that he was thankful. Yet, still, he missed the home he had, now gone. He gave out an involuntary whine.

***

Sid looked up from his book to watch Ben at the water's edge. He wondered when, not if, the big dog might take off on him and disappear. It wouldn't be unusual for a dog to look for a better deal. After all, Sid couldn't offer him much. He heard the dog's whine.

But the dog returned to the campsite with his wagging tail and sloppy tongue, then sat down near Sid's leg.

"Nap time?" Sid reached over to scratch Ben's ears. A few minutes later the dog was asleep.

***

He hadn't had the nightmare in some time, but even Ben

knew you can't pick and choose your dreams, especially the really bad ones.

It always started the same. He was a puppy, laying on his favorite blanket, staring into the fireplace. He was warm and the sound of crackles and pops was pleasant, relaxing. Often his people were also in the room, sitting on the couch, watching the fire with him.

There was playtime with toys and treats. There were always lots of balls to catch in the backyard.

Suddenly he was bigger, and he got to go to a park, with more balls to catch. Other dogs played, and his people laughed and talked.

The next thing he knew there were other sounds. He tried to get into the room where the sounds were coming from, but the door was always closed. The house was filled with shrill, loud noises, unpredictable, at all hours of the days and nights.

It was the smells that came with that sound that he remembered the most. Sweet smells, pleasant, like the flowers outside in the garden. They clung to the house, to the walls, and especially to the new blankets that had suddenly appeared. The blankets were small and soft, and Ben was curious, nosing his way towards them, until he was told to "Leave!" which he did.

After a time, Ben was allowed in the room, and closer to the blankets. He saw a wondrous thing: the tiniest person, squiggling and kicking. This was where the new sounds, and the new smells, came from. Fluffy things were all around, too, big fluffy things, small fluffy things. It looked wonderful.

It wasn't long before he knew the name of this person: Baybee. The word was used many times during the day.

"Hold the Baybee."

"Feed the Baybee."

"The Baybee is crying."

"The Baybee needs a nap."

He might not have understood all of those words, but he remembered the most important one: Baybee.

He would sit for the longest time just watching Baybee. In truth, sometimes it made other noises that weren't pleasant, and was often the cause of other smells that were very disgusting and made his eyes water, but one of the people always rushed around and got rid of the smells right away. Phew!

Then the nightmare truly began and Ben's heart began to beat harder.

One morning Ben was told to get outside, and he did, because he always did what he was told. But he sensed something bad. Fear, anger. Were they mad at him?

He wasn't allowed back inside the house all day. His food and water bowls were brought outside, and the door shut with a loud **Bang!**

Another day went by, then another. He was fed, given water, but little else. He slept on the ground. He had always slept in the house at night, in his bed. Until now.

A few days later, he was allowed back in by one of the people. The other one wasn't there, and he could not hear the Baybee, either. Some of the smell lingered. Cautiously he entered the room where the smells were always the strongest, but no, the blankets were gone, the fluffy things were gone. Where was Baybee?

The house was quiet.

But the other person came back and there was shouting and yelling and doors slamming. For a day. Maybe two. Or was it three? He tried to make his people happy, grabbing his ball and rolling it to their feet but each time the ball was kicked away, and then he was yelled at, too.

Ben now found that he *wanted* to be outside. And, *stay* outside. He slunk to the door, pawed at it, and waited. The door opened; Ben escaped to the peace of the back yard.

When he came inside the next day, the house was quiet. He wagged his tail, wanting to be told everything was all right. But it never really was and he never saw or heard or smelled Baybee again.

Always before, the nightmare was over and Ben could wake up. Not now. Now there was more.

***

Sid watched the big dog's muscle spasms and listened to his soft growls. Every few seconds he heard a throaty " Woofowolf." Do dogs dream? he wondered. He thought they might.

Ben's rear legs kicked as though he was running.

***

The nightmare seemed to go on and on. He was more afraid than he'd ever been. Ben was running. Running. Running. Running. Trying to catch a ball that could never be caught. He whimpered, then croaked another " Woofowolf!"

***

"This has gone on long enough," Sid said out loud, reaching over to shake the dog, rousing him awake. Ben's head jerked suddenly, his eyes still glazed from sleep. He looked at Sid and sat up.

"You OK, big boy?" Sid asked. He reached for a cookie. "Here, and I don't want no lectures that cookies are bad for you, either."

Ben took the offering and crunched through it before swallowing, then placed his head on one of Sid's legs.

"You're safe here," Sid stroked Ben's back. "I know what it's like to have bad dreams, especially the ones that never go away. I got me some of my own like that."

What happened to you? Sid wondered. *What did they do to you?*

They sat together, watching the river as the nearby hills absorbed the sun and wispy clouds turned pink and red before the sun disappeared.

CHAPTER ELEVEN
MR. AND MRS. LEE

D r. Sheila checked her email the first thing in the morning.

From: Liselle <liselleb@yournetwork.org>
To: Kaufman Vets

I think it should be illegal for a homeless person to own a dog. The dog didn't choose to be homeless, but it still has to suffer the consequences.

From: Doobydoo <dooby208@comail.com>
To: Kaufman Vets

Homeless people do not deserve to have pets, if they can't provide for themselves, they definitely can't provide for a pet. And these poor dogs have to stay outside 24/7 in rain or snow.

From: Shawman <Shawjones@mainstreet96.com>
To: Kaufman Vets

Are you going to take these dogs away from them? Pets are often the only happy things in their lives. Dogs can be a source of safety on the streets for these folks too. I'm sure wherever they sleep they keep each other warm.

Dr. Sheila puffed some air out of her cheeks. So much hatred from so many people. At least one person was sympathetic.

There was also a surprise:

From: S._Mannard <mannardbhet@service.com>
To: Kaufman Vets

I represent one of the largest service clubs in town. We're always looking for ways to help, and I think your program is great. Let me know, we can probably swing at least a thousand dollars your way.

***

"Rippers?" Dr. Jim asked his wife. He had worked late the night before and hadn't had the chance to hear his wife's report of her tour with Connie.

He finished suturing a cat's ear that had somehow got nicked. The wound wasn't deep and with some antibiotics the kitty would be able to go home with his anxious owner later that day.

"Connie said there have been incidents in other towns and cities. Vigilante types, calling themselves Rippers, taking matters into their own hands, raiding small homeless camps, tearing down tents and shelters. Making a mess of things."

Dr. Jim shook his head and placed the still- anaesthetized animal in a wire cage. "They can't defend themselves?"

"That's what's so ridiculous. They get stopped or

checked out by police sometimes and if they have weapons of any kind, even a table knife, they could be arrested. So, no, they can't defend themselves."

"A business owner wants to shoot homeless people with pellet guns but they can't shoot back."

Dr. Sheila put her head between her hands. "I thought I knew what this was all about. I've read newspaper articles and magazines. Pictures on the internet. But that's no substitute for actually going to their camps, meeting them.

"Connie said many weren't homeless a year ago, but they are now because of things they had no control over. They're from here, or nearby towns. Not from California, Texas, Florida, some other state. The newspapers never tell you that."

She took a deep breath. "I'm not sure we knew what we're getting into. We don't even have a location for the trailer yet."

Dr. Jim stepped over and put an arm around her shoulders. "We're not in this alone. The other veterinarians are going to help, and people from Denver will help, too. We just got another donation," reminding her of the email they had received. His words were reassuring.

"We're doing a good thing, you know that. And it's something we *need* to do."

One of their assistants opened the door and told them Mr. and Mrs. Lee were in the waiting room with two of their cats.

"Put them in Exam Room Four, please, I'll see them," Dr. Sheila told the assistant.

She sighed and stood up. "I just need to keep things in perspective," she smiled. "Taking care of regular clients will do that."

***

Mr. and Mrs. Lee placed small cat carriers on the examining room table. They were a retired couple, but looked younger than they were, perhaps because they were always upbeat and positive. They were involved in many community activities, both financially and as volunteers.

It seemed they always wore matching t-shirts with witty sayings, which elicited a smile from everybody they encountered. Today's matching message, appropriate for a trip to the veterinarian: "*We Brake for Strays.*"

They assiduously cared for several cats in their home, with an elaborate structure for them called a "catio." Today they were bringing in two young calicos they had adopted a few months before.

"These are stunning kitties," Dr. Sheila complimented, stroking the kittens in turn. Now out of their carriers, they were pleased with the attention, and purring loudly. Like most calicos, they were females, perhaps sisters, and bonded to each other.

Mrs. Lee beamed. "We couldn't be happier with them, they're such good babies."

"We want them spayed as soon as possible," Mr. Lee added. "But we want to make sure all of their vaccinations are up to date." He handed Dr. Sheila a file folder, inside were the kittens' medical records from the agency where they had been adopted.

She glanced at it, nodding her head. "Yes, everything's good. Six months old, they really should be spayed. Let's get that done."

She opened the door to call in an assistant. "Check our schedule, see if we can fit these two in next week for spays."

Mr. Lee said, "We read about the wonderful work you're doing for the homeless people. If you need help or volunteers," he nodded to his wife, "just let us know."

They turned to leave, but Mrs. Lee stopped. "I just had an idea. I don't know if you need a place for your set up, we own some property a few blocks from downtown. It's a paved parking lot with a small building. You can use it for free."

Mr. Lee nodded to his wife. "Oh, that's a great idea. We just lost our tenant a few days ago, he found a bigger place for his business. All the utilities are still on. You'll probably need electricity, right?"

"We're not in a hurry to lease it out again," Mrs. Lee added. "Why don't you look it over, see if it fits your needs. I'll text you the address."

Dr. Sheila's eyes grew wide, not sure if she believed what she had just heard. "Free? That is so generous of you. Thank you!"

The Lees smiled at her, then each other. "Glad to help any way we can," they said in unison.

Dr. Sheila couldn't wait to tell her husband.

Maybe this was going to work out after all.

CHAPTER TWELVE
WHAT ABOUT BEN?

Sid munched on an apple while Ben munched on his kibble. The sun was already over the river, slowly spreading lazy rays on the water.

When he first opened his eyes in the tent, the morning was cool. He stayed in his sleeping bag for some time, waiting until the tent warmed up. Ben lay close to his side, still asleep. He had let the big dog in last night, surprised he wanted in, surprised at himself for wanting him in.

He reached over to scratch Ben's ear. The dog rolled over, making a gruffing noise. "Not a morning person either, are you?" Sid smiled.

A short time later Sid nursed a cup of coffee next to the small fire he had re-kindled, thinking about what he should do.

The dog. Ben.

The thought was heavy and he needed to make plans.

He liked this town, some of its people, but it was going to get cold soon. He had to leave before the northern winds brought in rain, hail, and snow. Get ahead of it, don't delay, a lesson learned many years ago. No way was he going to wake up with snow on his tent. Been there, done that, and never again.

He watched Ben wander down to the river to lap up some water, walking back and forth along the bank before returning to Sid's side.

Sid chewed his lower lip. "We'll stop to see Tess first,

maybe there's word from the animal shelter," he said out loud.

He was still certain somebody was missing the dog, somebody was looking for him.

How could they not be?

He stroked Ben's neck and back, his hand returning several times to scratch the dog's head. The thought haunted him.

How could they not be? he asked himself again.

***

Ben watched Sid put out the small fire with some water, and kicked dirt into the ashes. What would they do today, he wondered. Yesterday had been so different from anything he had ever experienced. It was strange walking a long time — no bye-bye car! He'd also never been in a store before — so many smells he didn't recognize.

Sid was busy picking things up and clanking around, going back and forth. He wondered if he could help in some way, and decided the best thing to do right now was to stay out of the way but to keep a close watch, curious about what was next.

***

Decisions made, Sid began the work of breaking down his camp.

The light-weight aluminum frame of a backpack

appeared from a nearby bush. He pulled his sleeping bag out of the tent and rolled it into a tight roll. The tent was next, folded over and over into a compact square, the metal poles clanking together as he tied them up.

Several small pouches were filled with cooking utensils and the few clothes he carried for the road.

Sid was an old hand at this, he was quick and efficient. Ben's dog food added more weight than he liked, but perhaps that was temporary.

He'd be saying goodbye to the dog today at the shelter. Why did he feel such a pang in his stomach at that thought? The best place for Ben would be his own home. Another pang as he imagined Ben being led away. Why did he feel that way? *That makes no sense,* Sid thought. *I don't care how good a dog he is, I can't have him with me on the road, nope, can't have it.*

Within minutes the backpack was ready for him to shrug into. Before that happened, there was one more thing to do.

He stepped off into a nearby copse of junipers, turned right, then left, his eyes on the ground. Ben followed him.

"I'm not leaving ya," Sid said, reaching back to pet him.

He straightened up, then saw what he was looking for: A large rock about ten feet away. Sid bent down to scrape at the loose dirt at its base.

Seconds later he pulled out a small sack, and extracted several bills. Even though he knew how much was in it, he still counted it: Almost eight hundred dollars.

Under his shirt, around his waist, he unfastened an inconspicuous beige bag, an old money belt. This held a lesser amount, sixty dollars.

Among the many things Sid had learned over the years was once you settle down in an area for a while, never carry all of your money with you at the same time. You'd just be asking for trouble. Stash most of it away from prying or thieving eyes. This way, nobody ever knew how much money you have.

Of course, Sid never had a lot of money, but the few hundred dollars he had would be enough to buy food if he had no luck on a street corner, or pay a camping fee to pitch his tent, even get a cheap motel room if bad weather caught up to him.

He placed all of the bills back into his money belt, then returned to his camp.

Ben followed obediently, tail wagging, and watched as Sid bent his arms in the backpack's straps.

"Getting a little old for this," Sid groaned, then smiled at Ben and hooked the leash onto his collar. "Let's go."

***

Sid crossed the street in front of the grocery store, the dog following him. He shouldered out of his backpack and set it down by a brick planter.

Tess opened the front door for him. "You heading out already?" she asked him.

"You know me, hate the cold, getting a head start for warmer climes."

She bent down and patted Ben's neck. "He hasn't run off, yet."

"Nope, sticking close. Did you call the animal shelter?"

"Yes, twice yesterday and once this morning. No reports. And they're full, they can't take any more animals unless it's an emergency."

"And those internet things you were talking about?"

"Nothing on them either. But you're leaving now? What about Ben? What are you going to do?"

Sid shrugged and he shocked himself when he said, "I guess he can come with me a stretch, if he wants..." His words faded away as Ben looked up at him, eyes full of trust. "I guess," he repeated.

"There's always a possibility," Tess began but she stopped. She knew the chances for Ben's former owners to show up were now slim to none. She reached into the pocket of her apron. "Here's my card, maybe you can call me when you get to someplace, I might have news."

Sid smiled. "Well, payphones are few and far between now." They laughed together." And you know I don't have one of those cell phones."

Tess continued to laugh. "Maybe one day you'll join the rest of us in the twenty-first century and get one. Who knows? Stranger things have happened.

"Now let me get you a few things for the road," Tess began, but Sid shook his head.

"Can't carry much, my pack has to be light. I'm OK with what you gave me yesterday."

"This won't add to your load." Her tone was scolding. Oat bars, beef jerky, plus small packets of dried fruits and hard candies were swept into a paper sack which she handed to him.

Sid had always appreciated the store owner's kindness. She never asked him questions or pried about his past. She was a good person. He mumbled his thanks. "How about, when I get settled where I'm staying, I'll send you a postcard. If the owners turn up, they'll know where we're at." That was the best he could promise.

"See you next summer?" she asked.

"Count on it."

***

Tess watched Sid and Ben walk away. The state highway was a few streets to the west. It wouldn't take them long to reach it.

She heard the back door open and turned to see her teenage daughter, Becky, step in. "Got your day off?" she asked.

"Yep," Becky answered. Her red hair was in a long braid and she was wearing blue jeans and a short-sleeved shirt. "We still have to inspect the lines on the north range, we'll start that next week then we're done for the summer."

She grabbed some fresh apples and oranges. "Dad and I are going riding, haven't taken the horses out for a few days. Want to come?"

Tess shook her head. "Would love to, but I'm expecting a delivery from Jackson today."

Becky joined her mother at the window, peeling an orange. "Is that Sid? He's leaving already?" She had known the hitchhiker since she was a young girl, had seen him around town, knew he helped her mom from time to time with small chores and handy man kinds of things in the store. "Where's he going?"

"Arizona or New Mexico, Texas or Oklahoma." She hadn't asked, and Sid hadn't offered to tell her.

Becky frowned. "I didn't know he had a dog," she pointed at Ben.

"Two days ago, he didn't. Now he does."

"Hummmph. If I didn't know better that's the dog we found on the Old County Road." She turned to her mother. "Couple of days ago."

"What happened to it?"

"He was hot and thirsty, I gave him water and put him in the truck. Figured we'd get him to the animal shelter but that idiot Hal left the door open. The dog disappeared on us. His collar said his name was Ben."

Tess nodded. So, the dog *had* been dumped.

The phone rang and Becky said she'd answer it. "I wonder how that'll work out. Hitching rides with a big dog like that," Becky said over her shoulder.

Tess stepped out of the front door to get a better look at the receding figures. She had always worried about Sid. He had a harder life than a lot of homeless people; he was an easy target for ridicule and harassment. "Every time you leave here, I wonder if we'll see you again," she whispered.

She watched the dog prance happily along Sid's side, his head swinging this way and that.

Oh, Ben, do you know where you're going? Tess wondered. *Yes,*

Sid knows these roads. He's learned some hard lessons, but that's been his choice. Will you have to learn them, too?

Her thoughts echoed Becky's words. *I wonder how that'll work out.*

CHAPTER THIRTEEN
THE RIPPERS

ditty85:
We doing this? I gotta work today.

Magic:
Chill, bro, we'll get word

LouAxEm:
Yeah, Bryan will say

ditty85:
Do we have everything we need?

LouAxEm:
I got the masks, totally rad. Real scary, too. I'm gonna be a fox.

ditty85:
My dash cam's hooked up. And I got fireworks, too.

ditty85:
??? Fire crackers? What for, this ain't a party

Magic:
LOL. We gotta make a point.

LouAxEm:
Huh? What you mean?

LouAxEm:
Gotta scare em so they don't come back

ditty85:
Makes sense. They always come back

Magic:
Yeah, them always come back leaching off us, we work they don't. Get rid of em once and for all. Tired of it right?

ditty85:
Right

LouAxEm:
Right!!!

Magic:
In and out, they won't know what hit em

ditty85:
Hang loose, guys! This be happening.

CHAPTER FOURTEEN
CATCHING LUCK

Sid and Ben crossed over the two-lane state road. The morning was still cool so he decided to walk along the side. Several cars passed, the drivers paying him no mind.

"Now the trick is to be patient," Sid told Ben. "But luck has a lot to do with it, too. Catch some luck, catch some rides, is what I always say."

He had gone less than half a mile when he heard the approach of a large truck. This was the time to stick out his thumb.

"Why now?" he asked the dog, not expecting an answer. "Cuz my backpack is tall and hefty, it's too large for back seats of a regular car or inside trunks, and they'd have to make a longer stop on the shoulder of a narrow highway. No, folks ain't gonna do that for ol' Sid. But trucks of almost any size are better, my pack tossed in the bed — and we'll sit in the bed, too. Done that a lot of times. Can't be too proud, so you remember that."

Sid thought the truck, a large dual-axle, would go on by, but he got a surprise. The truck slowed, then stopped!

Sid hurried towards it, the driver got out. An older man, dressed in overalls.

"Let me help," he yelled, motioning Sid on. He took the pack and placed it in the bed. It was carrying a few bales of hay towards the back, there was plenty of room.

"You and the dog come on up. Getting' hot out here,

got the air conditioner goin' full blast."

Sid went around to the passenger side, Ben followed and jumped up into the back cab as instructed. Sid belted himself in on the passenger side.

"Sure appreciate this," he said.

"I'm going as far as the next county crossing, about 70 miles. Nice dog you got there," the driver said, steering the truck back onto the highway. "A golden, right? What's his name? I had a dog just like that when I was a kid, best dog I ever had, too." He glanced back. Ben was sitting by the window, looking at the passing country side with avid interest. "Lucky man has a dog like that, yessir, lucky man."

Sid wasn't about to argue. Catch luck, catch a ride.

***

Ben looked out the window at the passing scenery. This was so different than anything he had ever experienced. Before, going bye-bye was always exciting because he was going to play and run and jump. But here? He heard his name a couple of times.

Almost before he knew it, Sid was telling him to get out of the truck, but a few minutes later, here was another truck! Another window to look out of. He heard Sid say his name again. It didn't seem to make any sense, but Ben decided it was all OK.

***

They made good time. They never had to sit in the bed of a truck, either, always invited into the cab, and everyone gave them ice-cold water from an ice chest.

Two younger women in an SUV picked them up. They were on their way back home to Denver after a week in Yellowstone. They were friendly, chatty, and obviously interested in dogs in general, Ben in particular.

A couple from Salt Lake City picked them up, their truck pulling a fifth wheel. Loved Ben, and they decided then and there their twin grandchildren would get a golden for their birthdays.

By now Sid was mildly amused that *everybody* who picked them up had either once had a dog "just like Ben" or wanted a dog "just like Ben."

At this rate, they would be at the state line tomorrow, a hitch-hiking' trip that might normally take three or even four days.

***

Early that evening, Sid led Ben off the road through a break in the shrubs and trees. This spot was dense with rabbit brush and scrawny junipers.

They took a narrow trail that was easy to ignore and difficult to find. He unclipped Ben, letting him lead the way. The dog bounded forward, sniffing every bush.

Sid took this trail whenever he could while traveling the state road back and forth. It led to a narrow canyon, and a spot where Sid could truly be alone, away from anybody and everybody. Peace and quiet for a night. He liked to explore, this way and that, the cliffs and shady ravines, looking for something new, perhaps a surprise.

Like now.

They rounded a curve on the trail and a few hundred feet in front of them was a band of horses. Sid immediately stopped, and held his breath. Would Ben try to chase them?

But the dog also stopped, his eyes wide.

A stallion turned to look at them. He was tall, dark brown with splashes of white across his back and chest. His gaze left no doubt he was in charge here. He snorted, perhaps as a warning.

Two mares stood behind him, one a dappled gray, the other a black and white pinto. Sid held his breath when movement from behind them caught his eye. Two colts peered out from behind the mares' long legs. The coat of one of the colts was pure white, the other was brown and white like his father.

Ben turned his head slightly to look back at Sid, and that movement was enough for the stallion to give a silent message to his family. In three blinks of an eye, they disappeared down the trail, leaving only dust clouds where they had once stood.

"That was something, wasn't it," Sid whispered.

Ben's tail wagged as though he agreed, his eyes still wide.

A few hundred feet on was a large depression at the base of a cliff. In the spring, the depression would be full of water, fed by a waterfall cascading from a hundred feet above. This time of year, the pond was dry, but shade from nearby cottonwoods hugged the afternoon's light.

Sid found a place to sit and opened up a fruit bar. The ground was soft and sandy. There was no need to pitch his tent, he would just roll out his sleeping bag and watch the sky turn dark and stars come out.

Sid watched Ben explore the area, the dog disappearing every few seconds behind bushes or trees. He found a steep game trail and was making his way up and up.

Too far up.

Sid's heart skipped a beat.

***

Ben climbed and climbed, jumping over rocks and mounds of dirt. He had never been in a place like this, so many sounds and smells. He stopped every few feet to sniff at branches and leaves. He sensed there were little animals watching him in their hiding places.

He was on a ledge now and could see Sid a long way down. He hadn't realized he had climbed so high! A cool breeze ruffled his fur and he turned to look down the canyon, the sun in his eyes.

How far can I go? he wondered. *How far have I come?* The thoughts were thrilling, enticing.

I have never been so happy in my life.

He heard Sid call to him, "Come on down. Time for supper. Be a good boy, Ben."

***

Did it seem to Sid that the dog paused for a few seconds after he called for him? His heart tumbled.

Oh, no, this would not be the place for him to disappear, in the middle of nowhere...

Would the dog come down, come back to him?

He watched Ben turn around and begin to climb down from the hill.

Without understanding the relief he felt, Sid willed his heart back to normal.

Ben was coming back to him.

***

Night was settling in. Sid ate his last sandwich from Tess, gave Ben the last bit of it, then ruffled the fur on his neck. "Please. Always come back to me, won't you?" Sid asked.

***

I hope Sid knows how much I like being here, being with him, Ben thought.

I really liked the bit of sandwich he just gave me. I'll put my head on his shoulder, I hope he doesn't mind that.

***

The pair listened to the distant rustling of birds in trees. There were other sounds, soft and close, not alarming, just small animals doing what they had to do in the dark.

Sid noticed deer tracks in the sand but knew they wouldn't come close. Rodents might, so he kept his shoes in his sleeping bag. The laces would be particularly appealing to packrats.

There was no evidence that anybody else had found the spot, no sign of campfires, tents, or trash. For years, it had been his, and his alone. For somebody like Sid, it was perfect.

But this time, he wasn't alone. He had Ben.

"You want the first watch, or should I?" Sid asked the dog, chuckling. The dog tilted his head and gave him a goofy smile.

"OK, I'll go first."

CHAPTER FIFTEEN
SHOULD WE BRING GUNS?

Tonight was a meeting of local veterinarians as plans were finalized for their mobile clinic.

Dr. Jim gave them a financial update. "With the extra donations, we've got all of the funding we need."

"That's surprising," one of the veterinarians said, "especially the town government matching that twenty-five thousand."

Dr. Jim smiled. "My wife was very persuasive."

There was laughter all around.

Dr. Sheila appreciated the humor. "I want to make sure I answer everybody's questions tonight, or at least try. I met with the county's homeless advocate, her name is Connie, and we went to one of their camps. She gave me a lot of information.

"But the big news! We have a great place to set up. Free!" This was met with excited murmurs.

She went on to explain there was enough money for at least two weekends, spread out over a month. "We might have money for one more, but we'd have to make sure the trailer is available."

Dr. Jim handed out copies of the budget. "We think we've covered everything, but please look this over, make sure we haven't missed anything."

Months before, in the early planning stages, there had been agreements that the veterinarians would volunteer their time and services, but they could not in good conscience ask their assistants to do the same, so they would be paid their usual salary, plus additional for the weekend hours. Twenty assistants for each weekend would be required.

Anesthesia and vaccinations were also budget items. One of the veterinarians reported she had obtained 100 free vials of distemper vaccine from her supplier.

"That helps a lot," Dr. Jim nodded. "I'll adjust the budget."

Bandages, sutures, disinfectant, and various other items were also listed.

"All of the pet stores are going to donate free bags of dog food, leashes, toys, anything like that to give away," one of the other veterinarians told them.

"But," he added, "I have a question, and maybe I shouldn't bring this up, but I have to." He was a younger vet and had recently joined one of the other hospitals.

"Go ahead," Dr. Sheila encouraged, then almost immediately regretted it when she heard his question.

"Look, all I know about these people is what I've read in the papers or seen on TV. Is this going to be dangerous? I mean, should I bring a gun or something? Would that be a good idea?"

There was a ripple of nervous laughter but it was obvious a couple of the others had the same question because they were nodding in agreement.

Dr. Sheila blinked, bit her lip. *These people.* Connie's words came back to her: *I try not to judge.*

She chose her words carefully but kept a friendly tone.

"That's a good question. Like a lot of you, I've been wondering about our safety, too. After meeting with Connie, a lot of things cleared up in my mind. They aren't dangerous, in fact they're just as frightened of us as we are of them. Some have serious problems, but many of them weren't homeless a year or two ago. They had jobs, families, husbands, wives. But things happened in their lives they couldn't control, or they didn't get help in time before they lost everything.

"What's relevant to us is that a number of them have dogs." She shrugged. "And no matter what anybody thinks about that, it's just a reality. But we can help. We deserve a lot of credit."

Everybody nodded.

"However," Dr. Sheila continued, making eye contact with the veterinarian who had asked about guns. "I think you have a legitimate concern. I'll ask if there's a possibility a sheriff's deputy could patrol our location a few times a day when we're there. Actually, I think that's a pretty good idea."

Pastor Larry's words came back to her:
There's fear on both sides.

***

The meeting broke up a few minutes later. "I notice you didn't tell them about those awful emails — or the 'Rippers,'" Dr. Jim said to his wife.

She grunted. "I figured that was a bridge too far for some of them. I mean," she said with some sarcasm. "I don't want

ALL of them to be packing heat."

CHAPTER SIXTEEN
"THAT'S SOME DOG"

Sid broke camp just after dawn. Ben ate his kibble while Sid ate a fruit bar. An hour later, they were back on the state road and almost immediately got a ride.

The driver of an older pickup truck was a woman who proceeded to tell a sad story about "a dog like yours, she got cancer. I miss her, but she's in a good place."

A larger commercial van owned by an independent delivery company was next. "They don't like me picking up hitch hikers, but hey what they don't know, I don't care." he said. "Have two big dogs, an Irish Setter and a black lab, goofiest things you ever saw, run for miles and never get tired. Eat like horses. Bet your dog does, too, right?"

They were close to the state line. "This is as far as I go, don't have a license to deliver beyond here," the driver told him. He slowed to a stop, Sid retrieved his backpack and Ben jumped down through the van's double doors. Sid thanked him, then took to the wide shoulder.

***

State highways are little more than paved roads, often only two lanes, sometimes with passing lanes, usually not, the black tar asphalt sometimes well maintained, usually not.

This state highway was no different and by early

afternoon it was a hot, steamy black slash against a lonely landscape.

Sid knew this section of road. Winding and twisting, it was narrow in spots with a scant shoulder and a steep drop off on one side, a high embankment on the other. Deer were common on this stretch, coming and going from nearby hills and canyons. Drivers frequently went too fast and the predictable occurred many times a week. Brakes screeched, the animals smashed into grills of large trucks, flailing legs skipping over hoods and tops of small cars.

Drivers were lucky if they escaped without serious injury or worse.

The deer never were.

***

Sid and Ben rounded a bend. Two trucks and a car were parked on the side in a hap-hazard way.

Off the road, a small passenger car was a-tilt on its side, its hood crumpled into where the windshield once was. Broken glass littered the ground. Further down the embankment, at the bottom of a shallow gully, lay the body of a deer, a small doe.

Sitting on the pavement next to the stopped car was a young woman. Her right arm was akimbo, probably broken. She had a nasty gash near her neck. A woman was pressing a piece of cloth to it, trying to stop the bleeding.

The accident victim was trying to talk. "But…please…" her voice came out in a croak.

"Don't you try to talk, sweetie. We called 911. An ambulance will be here in just a few minutes."

Two men stood nearby, looking at the damaged car. "Whoa," one of them said, pointing. "There it goes." The car began to slide down the embankment into the gully.

"Come here, boy," Sid told Ben. He pulled the leash out from his back pocket and clicked it on the collar.

"Best you stay by me." He was intent on getting to the other side of the road, and move on. This was none of his business.

Ben twirled around, resisting the leash. He whined, and jerked hard, forcing it out of Sid's hand. He ran as fast as he could, down the embankment, towards the car.

He heard Sid shout his name but nothing, *nothing,* could stop him. He hurled himself at the car door.

***

The smell. That familiar, wonderful smell. Yes, that was it, he could never forget it, he was a half rememberin' half forgettin' dog, after all, and the rememberin' half would *never* forget that smell!

Baybee was in here, right here!

He wagged his tail, ran to the other side of the car, and barked as loud as he could.

***

The bystanders shouted at the dog. What if the car slid

in the soft dirt? So what? It was badly damaged, the wrecker would just have more of a job getting it out of the gully.

The young woman gasped, trying to crawl towards the car. The older woman restrained her. "It's just a car, nothing you can do about it."

***

Ben was furious and growled. *Why aren't they listening to me?* He ran back and forth from one end of the car to the next.

It kept sliding, dirt and rocks tumbling with it.

***

Sid was frantic, Ben was on the wrong side of that car! Another man was at his side, shouting. "What is that dog thinking?"

Ben gave out a "Woofowolf" deep in his throat.

***

What was it about that sound? Sid wondered. He had heard it before. He craned his neck to see Ben, who had disappeared to the other side of the car.

"My dog…" he pointed to Ben, getting the attention of the man. "He wouldn't be doing that unless something…"

Something what, *what?*

Sid's instinct took over. He threw off the backpack into

the dirt, then scurried down to the car. Another man, burly and a little over-weight, followed him, sending down a cascade of dirt and gravel.

***

I'll start to bark, really loud, and race around the car, that's what I'll do! Ben skidded to a stop when he saw Sid.

Yes! Come now! Yes! Right here! Baybee is inside, Baybee is inside.

***

The car continued to slide.

Ben barked, furious and impatient. Sid opened the rear door.

Sid now saw why Ben was frantic. An infant car seat loomed in his vision. A baby, deep in a blue blanket, was in it, an array of straps crisscrossing each other over the tiny body. Sid willed the car to stop, he needed time.

The man next to Sid huffed, "Oh, no…"

No time! With clicks and a jerk, Sid dislodged the carrier from its frame and pulled it out. It was heavy and awkward. Sid struggled to keep his balance. Bracing it against a knee, he tried to get up the slope, back to the road. He couldn't do it.

"Can you take it?" he asked the other man who was still near the corner of the car. The man nodded, grabbed the carrier, turned, but almost fell backwards. Sid reached out to brace him. The man regained his footing and reached the top.

Sid climbed up the bank on all fours, Ben following him closely.

"Oh, my heavens," the older woman yelled as she ran down to help. The man handed the carrier to her. The woman quickly put it on the ground then unstrapped the infant, his bright blue eyes looking around. An instant later he was next to his mother, who was crying from relief and gratitude.

***

Ben lifted his head up and tried to look in the carrier, but it was handed over to another person. A tiny being was lifted out and handed to the person sitting on the road. The smell that Ben knew so well lingered in the air.

He looked at Sid with a happy grin. *There's a tiny person, maybe it's MY tiny person. It's Baybee, right?*

***

"Are you OK, Ben?" Sid asked. He kneeled down to feel the dog's legs, lifting his paws to see if any rocks or gravel might have hurt them. "You're a good boy, Ben, such a good boy," he muttered, breathless from what had just happened.

The woman turned and for a moment looked at Sid, but quickly looked away to the other man, the one who had taken the carrier from Sid. "I don't think I've ever seen

GOOD BOY BEN

anything like that. Lucky you came along," she gushed.

The man stepped around, a big grin on his face as he accepted more praise and slaps on his back.

Ignored, Sid picked up his backpack. He called to Ben but turned to watch the car continue its slide, landing on its side with a thud of metal and breaking glass as it hit rocks. The crowd gasped, watching it tumble over and over, the roof demolished.

"If that baby had still been in there..." somebody said.

They heard a siren, then another, faint but getting closer. Sid grabbed Ben's leash and crossed the road in a hurry. He had no interest in staying around longer.

They weaved their way around other vehicles that had also stopped. A man and woman emerged from a truck.

"Wait," the woman shouted to Ben. "We saw what happened. We're going as far as the Interstate, a hundred miles. We have lots of room." She smiled down at Ben. "That's some dog you got there.

"We have one just like him at home."

CHAPTER SEVENTEEN
CHANGE

Sid was familiar with this town, had often passed through but never stayed long. It was a little large for his taste, and there was too much competition for both handouts and odd jobs. There were always a lot of changes, new buildings and shopping malls going up.

Ben was on his leash, tail wagging, tongue lolling out of his mouth as usual. They crossed a wide median to the other side of the four-lane highway.

Sid's destination was an older, well-established RV park. The owner welcomed over-night tent campers (thirty dollars a night); allowed the use of the showers (fifteen dollars a day, plus ten dollars for soap, shampoo, and towels); and the laundromat (eight quarters for one washing machine, ten quarters for one dryer, iron and ironing board available).

Dogs were welcome.

He passed a myriad of RVs and truck campers of various sizes and quality, some new, some old, but all parked in neat rows with picnic tables and chairs outside on smooth concrete patios. A few RV owners sitting in plastic chairs waved to him (or, were they actually waving at Ben, Sid wondered with a smile. Probably Ben).

The large office was mid-way into the park. Sid stepped into air-conditioned comfort and made his way to the counter. Colorful brochures lined a nearby wall and a rack of postcards (five dollars each), stood on the other side of the room. A well-worn leather couch and several chairs were near a window.

Val, the owner, came out of a small room when she heard the door open. She immediately recognized Sid.

"Wondered when I'd see you. Seems you're a little early."

Sid had been stopping here for a night or two for some years, he was a regular.

"Was looking to get cold up north," he explained, "didn't mind getting a head start."

She nodded to Ben. "That's a big dog, a lot bigger than others I see with your kind."

Your kind. Sid knew she didn't mean it as an insult, and he didn't take it that way. "He was a surprise," he agreed. "Didn't expect to have no dog. Ever. His name's Ben."

She opened a ledger, assiduously kept to record everyone who came and went. "If you're staying a couple of days, I have some deck chairs need staining before winter. I can give you a free night if you're interested. I'll also give you breakfast, both mornings."

He had been thinking about leaving in the morning, but breakfasts and a free night were too good to pass up.

He gave her enough money for his one paid night and tokens for showers, then turned to leave. Val's next words stopped him.

"I suppose I should tell you, I'm selling the place. Getting too old. Finally retiring to Florida. But..." she tilted her head, suddenly sympathetic. She let the other shoe drop, clipping her words. "New owners not going to allow folks off the road anymore. Gotta have wheels."

Sid grimaced. "Sorry to hear that, but I'm glad for you. You've had this park a long time."

"Most of my life, it seems. I'm gettin' on seventy now and figured I'd better try to enjoy some of my life."

She handed him a key to the shower, and a few plastic bags, "for Ben."

He took them and turned to leave. "Thanks for your help," he told her, and meant it. The RV park had been a good resting place for him, safe and pleasant. He would miss it.

***

It took Sid only a few minutes to find his spot, set up his tent, and stash his few belongings (leaving his money belt securely around his waist) before zipping up the opening. He gave Ben some water, then eased himself into a chair a few feet away on the lawn. There was plenty of daylight left and now he could sit and relax for a time, and think.

He wouldn't do any panhandling here, he decided. He'd be gone before anybody took notice of him and that was fine. Val had given him sour news and he wanted to get out of this town and might never come back. There were other highways he could hitch rides on, and he knew all of them.

Sid thought about the route he'd be taking to get out of here in two days. He didn't need a map, it was etched in his mind.

He and Ben would hitch rides up to the Colorado mountains, stay a few days in one of the ski towns with super huge homes built for super rich people who didn't live there but might show up for a week or two a year. Towns that also had aged hippies who didn't give so much as a second glance to him or his backpack. Towns where people were generous with their handouts.

He'd do some grocery shopping there, just a few items to get him by, but certainly dog food for Ben.

He'd pitch his tent in some camping spots he knew of, as they made their way down to the southern edge of the state. Maybe go straight on into New Mexico. Maybe take a hard right into Arizona. Maybe take a hard left into Oklahoma then on to Texas. Maybe by the end of next week, or the week after, he'd be where he wanted to be for the winter.

Almost every year he could make these decisions easily. He had only himself, after all. Now he had Ben.

He looked at the dog, reached down to stroke his long fur.

A responsibility. Somebody else to look out for, to feed. Make sure he was safe.

Once again, he asked himself why he hadn't left him, walk away. They had shelters in this town, maybe they had room. He could just leave him, maybe somebody would give him a home.

Leave him. The two words stuck like a sour piece of candy.

His heart and gut twisted at the same time. No, he couldn't do that, especially after today. This dog was smart, straight as an arrow when his mind was made up.

He had seen that at the accident, the look in his eyes, frantic to get Sid's attention.

Even though it had been some hours ago, Sid knew his adrenaline was still high. Watching that car slide, trying to get Ben to come back to him, discovering the baby. All in the span of a few seconds.

That's how these things happened. Quick, no time to think, only react. Or, like a lot of people do, freeze in panic and indecision.

Sid hadn't frozen. But, then, neither had Ben. The peculiar whine the dog had made was the same sound he had made when he was asleep, tortured by that nightmare. It was beyond understanding why Sid had known Ben was trying to tell him something.

He shook his head, leaned back, forced himself to relax, take it easy.

Be good to yourself.
Be good to Ben.

***

Ben was also thinking about the day, how he had smelled his Baybee. All he wanted to do was see the Baybee again, it had been such a long time. Would Baybee remember him? Would they go back to the house where they lived, with the big back yard, and his own food bowl, and riding in the bye-bye car to the park?

But had it been *his* Baybee? Were there more than one of them? That was confusing.

What was more confusing were the questions Ben now asked himself. Did he actually *want* to see his Baybee again? Did he *want* to go back to the house? That last ride in the bye-bye car didn't turn out so well, did it.

Those were some serious things to think about.

***

Since Sid had a free night in exchange for some work, he felt like splurging just a little. There were several fast-food places nearby, and he had a yen for Mexican food. He left the park with Ben on leash.

Fifteen minutes later he was sitting on a picnic table outside the restaurant, enjoying four tacos, a large soda, and a side of nacho chips. He didn't do this very often, so when he did, it was a treat. He slipped Ben a chip from time to time, the dog happily crunched them. "But no cheese," Sid chuckled, "unless you sleep outside the tent."

The dog looked up at him as though he was laughing, too.

Walking back to the park he took a different route, a few streets over, just to get away from the busy highway. It wasn't as noisy, but still lined with strip malls and convenience stores. Small areas of grass and scraggly trees broke up the parking lots.

A sign announcing **Good Meadows Shelter**, was near the sidewalk. He glanced at the building. Several men stood outside, some talking, some smoking. He knew what they were.

Homeless. He straightened his back and kept a firm grip on Ben's leash, making sure that he would not, could not, be mistaken for any of them. He was just a guy with a dog, heading for the RV park. Passing through. Not worth paying attention to.

He quickly cut across the parking lot, putting as much distance between him and the homeless as he could.

CHAPTER EIGHTEEN
TEAMS

C lassy was always "up and at 'em" as soon as the sun rose.

She pawed at Ryan, who was still sleeping. She could see only the top of his head in the soft material that covered him. She jumped on him, whining, wagging her short tail.

Finally, she heard a grunt. Success! Ryan pulled out a hand and gave her a rigorous head scratching, then sat up and reached for the opening of the balloon they now called home.

Classy ran outside. The morning air was cool. She headed for a small pond a few hundred feet away to get a drink of water. She sniffed the air, the sour odor of campfire smoke lingering nearby.

At the pond's edge were several ducks which she cheerily routed. "Go away!" she told them and even though they couldn't understand her words, they understood her barks, so they obeyed, flapping their wings and squawking.

The last few weeks of her life had been confusing. Before, she'd had a nice bed all her own with lots of toys and a big back yard with trees and grass. More importantly, there were several people who paid her lots of attention. Pettings and good food and lots of warm laps to jump in and get cuddled.

But it was Ryan who she loved more than anybody. It was Ryan who had given her those toys and made sure she was in her bed at night, and took her for lots of walks down quiet streets during the day. She made friends with a few of the dogs behind fences, stopping to say hi, or talk to them for a few minutes.

Her bed, her toys, the back yard, all were gone now. At least there were dogs here in their new home, and a lot of them were helpful and nice.

She watched as one of them, Brutus, walked down to the pond's edge. He was an oldster like her, a little gruff, but Classy liked him a lot. He was an admirable dog.

"Morning," he said, lapping at the water.

"Morning," she answered, happy to have somebody to talk to.

He yawned and stretched. "Sure was hot yesterday." He looked around. "Maybe we can stay in the camp today." He and his owner didn't have a balloon, instead staying in a rusty box that never moved.

"That would be great. Maybe we can stay, too," Classy said, but she doubted it. Ryan liked to leave this place during the day.

"We had a good supper last night, my person gave me hamburgers." Brutus burped a little, then stretched his legs.

"I like hamburgers! We had hot dogs." Classy tried to

burp, too, but she couldn't make a big sound like Brutus could.

By then a couple of other dogs were heading to the pond, and some people, too. She heard Ryan call her name and she scampered back to the camp.

Where would they go today, she wondered. It was always an adventure, always different, and they were always together.

She loved Ryan, and he loved her.

We're a team!

***

Sid checked in with Val before starting on the chairs. She told him they were in the big barn near the back of the park. "Use whatever you need. Here're some bottles of cold water, too. It's going to be hot today."

She reached down to stroke Ben and laughed. "Are you going to help him?" she asked the dog.

"Oh, he'll help all right," Sid joined in the joke. "We make a good team."

***

Dr. Sheila drove her car into the vacant lot that Mr. and Mrs. Lee had offered for the veterinary trailer. Connie was already there.

"This is a good location," Connie said as they began to walk around the property. "A few blocks from our largest homeless camp, close but not too close. And we can use it all of the dates you have planned?" Connie asked. "Free? That's very generous."

Dr. Sheila nodded. "Mr. and Mrs. Lee said we can use it as many weekends as we want."

They took note of several exterior plug-ins as well as a canopy on the side of the building. "We can set up chairs back here," Dr. Sheila said. "People can rest and wait their turn."

Dr. Sheila had a key to the building. She flicked on the lights. A long, gleaming counter was near the front door.

"It's really clean," Connie noticed.

"We can use this to take breaks, maybe even store some of our supplies." She opened a small refrigerator near the counter. "Some medications need to be kept cold," she mumbled.

They stepped back outside a few minutes later. Dr. Sheila locked the door behind her.

"I think we're ready to set up some dates, ask the Denver clinic if those are open for the trailer," Dr. Sheila said. "Then we'll start to get the word out. We'll print some flyers."

Connie nodded. "The churches will help with that, and some of the more, uh, friendly store owners, too."

They laughed.

Connie said, "I'll text you if I come up with any questions or ideas." She paused before getting into her SUV. "We make a good team, don't we."

The veterinarian beamed. "Yes, we do."

***

Sid found the three chairs needing refinishing in the work barn near the back of the RV property. It was large, containing tools and maintenance equipment such as trimmers, hedge clippers, chain saws, and a riding lawnmower.

Sid suspected the chairs needed more than "just" refinishing and he was right. Old paint would need to be removed, some sanding required, before stain could be applied. The RV park owner knew Sid would do the job, and do it right, without complaint.

Ben plopped down inside the barn out of the hot sun, ready to watch Sid, but mostly ready to take a nap.

"Hey!" Sid reproached the dog. "I thought you said you were going to help. Some team we are."

Ben grunted and rolled over onto his side.

Sid chuckled. He spread a drop cloth under the chairs, grabbed a wire brush, some sandpaper, and went to work.

Ben went to sleep.

***

Bryan
Dudes. It's on. We're doing this tomorrow

ditty85:
Dija get Magic's message? He's out.

LouAxEm:
What u mean?

ditty85:
Kid's sick. Some lame excuse

Bryan
It's cool. We'll hit a smaller camp. Just the three of us. It'll be like a test run, practice, you know?

LouAxEm:
You sure? I mean we planned on all of us.

Bryan
We got this. The video will be awesome, we're gonna be FAMOUS!

ditty85:

LET'S GO TEAM!!!

LouAxEm:

LET'S GO TEAM!!!

Bryan

LET'S GO TEAM!!!

CHAPTER NINETEEN
JUST BREATHE

Sid was ready to leave the RV park. He had taken an early morning shower and washed the few clothes he had in the laundromat, knowing it might be three or four days before he could to that again.

He looked down at Ben, and ruffled up the fur around his neck. "Ready to go?" The dog pranced around as the leash was clipped on.

Val was sweeping off the sidewalk in front of her office. He waved to her but didn't stop. She knew he was leaving; he knew he wouldn't see her again.

***

Ryan stood on a street corner with a sign for almost an hour but had nothing to show for it. Maybe it was getting too hot for folks to slow down or stop to hand him a buck. He needed to leave anyway, his inhaler was almost empty and he needed to get a new one. It wasn't a prescription, but he could get a cheap generic one at the grocery store. He had just enough money to buy it, and maybe some candy.

Classy followed him as he began to walk the short distance to the store. He had his pack strapped to his back, it didn't hold much, but he'd have to leave it outside the store, couldn't take it in with him.

He knew a place, a safe place, that was used by friends he'd made at the homeless camp to leave their packs, sacks, or carts. At least, they said it was safe.

***

Sid didn't want to chance the big, busy highway interchange, there wasn't a good place to stand or a good place where a vehicle could or would stop. He decided to stay to the side streets instead, make his way over the railroad tracks, around the interchange, to eventually meet up with the highway on the other side. It would take longer, but when was he ever in a hurry anyway?

***

Ryan took off his small pack and placed it against a wall. He saw there were several other bags and packs already there, and a few cell phones plugged into an electrical outlet. Yes, a safe place that everybody knew about.

He looked up at the sign over the door. **Good Meadows Shelter**, it read, and beneath it in block letters: *Good nights and welcoming meals for all.*

The grocery store was in the next shopping mall. He picked Classy up and carried her in, ignoring the stares and critical looks. He didn't care. She went where he went. Always and period.

He quickly found the inhaler, then picked up a small bag of chocolates a few aisles over. He bypassed a clerk and used the self-checkout, paying it with a twenty-dollar bill, getting back only a few dollars and some change. It was almost all the money he had.

He would have to find some work, and soon. The inhaler, in this heat, would last only a few days.

Still carrying Classy, he sauntered back to the building where his pack was.

And stopped.

Wait, this was wrong. He stared at the sign, no, this was the building. He looked around, his mind exploding with confusion.

His pack, actually, all of the other bags and packs were gone.

All of the cell phones were gone, too!

He dropped his grocery sack.

***

Sid and Ben paused on a grassy break in the pavement under a large tree. The shade felt good. He hoped they could get a ride quickly when they hit the highway, he did not relish standing in the hot sun. Maybe getting such an early start this year had been a bad idea, maybe should have stayed up north for a few more weeks. Too late now.

The homeless shelter loomed in front of him. He hurried to walk around it, but he heard a haunting, keening sound.

Near the front, a young man, a boy, really, was holding a small dog and running back and forth, back and forth, and began to pound on the doors.

***

Dr. Sheila stepped out of the hospital into the hot sun; the pavement from the parking lot seemed to be steaming. It had to be close to a hundred already, she thought.

She had a break in her appointments and wanted to get an early lunch before the surgeries scheduled for that afternoon. She promised Jim she'd bring him back something to eat.

Her favorite Chinese food restaurant was nearby and despite the heat she decided to walk. She passed the stores and the strip mall, cutting across a parking lot, then kept to the sidewalk that skirted the large building that housed the homeless shelter. It had large double doors in the front but no windows. Dr. Sheila remembered what Connie had said. Social services hadn't inspected it yet.

She heard a commotion. Somebody was yelling in obvious distress.

***

Ryan was frantic. Where was his bag? His clothes, food for Classy, his music player. Everything was in there. Why would somebody take it? He was furious, his fists bunched up as he pounded on the glass doors.

"Hey! Is somebody in there? Hey!"

Ryan felt his chest expand, then contract. He was getting a headache. And he knew what that meant. He doubled over in pain, let go of Classy, and scrambled for the paper sack that held his new inhaler.

***

Sid held Ben's leash tightly, he just wanted to walk past, not get involved. But then he saw the boy collapse in front of the door.

***

Classy whined, jumped over Ryan's body, but stayed with him. She had seen her person do this before.

***

Dr. Sheila ran across the parking lot. She recognized

Ryan from the church give-away, and she recognized the signs. He was having an asthma attack, a bad one.

She reached him just as he fell, his hand gripping the inhaler.

"Let me help you."

She saw the tall man with the Golden Retriever standing a short distance away. She motioned to him and raised her voice. "Can you help? I need to get him in a sitting position. Please."

***

Sid could keep walking, just like he could have kept walking two days ago on the state road, kept a tighter grip on Ben's leash, ignore that accident. Yes, he could have hurried away, unnoticed and unimportant.

But he hadn't.

And today? He could take Ben, ignore that woman's pleas and the boy's distress, cross to the other side of the street, unnoticed and unimportant.

But he didn't.

***

Sid quickly unshouldered his backpack and helped the woman get the boy into a sitting position.

"You're Ryan, aren't you?" the woman asked. The boy nodded.

"His color doesn't look too good," Sid murmured.

"Here," the woman said. "Breathe. Deep and slow. Just breathe."

CHAPTER TWENTY
LOST TIME

Dr. Sheila held the inhaler to Ryan's mouth. "That's good. Take it easy." She was struck by how young he was. She remembered what Pastor Larry had said, a teenager. Fragile, vulnerable.

"Are you a doctor?" Sid asked.

She shook her head. "Veterinarian. But...well, there are some cross-overs." She shrugged. "I know the symptoms."

She fished Connie's card out from her purse and called the number. Connie answered on the second ring; Dr. Sheila briefly explained what had happened.

"I'm on my way," the social worker said.

***

Ben sat a few feet away from Sid, watching what was happening to the people, but was more interested in the little dog who kept whining and pacing back and forth.

"Hey," he called to it, "want to come over here?"

The dog stopped. "I guess. What's your name?"

"Ben. Who are you?" He knelt down on his stomach to meet Classy one-on-one at her own level.

"I'm a no good-for-nothing-furball-silly-little-terrier."

"Why would you say that?" Ben flared his ears.

"Because that's what humans say about me," Classy replied. She didn't sit down, but kept looking over at Ryan. "Except him, he named me Classy."

"Well, gotta say, that's a much better name."

"I like it, too."

"Is he going to be all right?"

"I think so, he always is after this sort of thing happens."

***

Ryan was able to sit up on his own, but with some effort. He was embarrassed, he'd never had to have somebody's help for quite a while but realized this episode was serious.

"Thanks, I'm OK now, didn't mean to be no trouble." He spotted Classy and called to her. She immediately came over and sat on his lap.

"You're no trouble," Dr. Sheila assured him. She looked up at Sid. "We're happy to help. I'm Dr. Sheila and this is…" she tilted her head, looking at the stranger.

"Sid," was the brisk response. He indicated the front door. "Did you stay here last night?"

Ryan shook his head. "No, they don't allow dogs. And shelters, well, they fill up real fast. By the time I get around to it, they don't have any beds left. That's OK, I have a tent down by the gravel pit. A lot better for me and my girl here."

He ruffled Classy's fur. "But I don't know what I'm going to do, they took my pack…and a lot of other people's stuff, too." He remained sitting, too weak to stand up.

Dr. Sheila frowned, confused.

Sid understood why. "If you're homeless, sometimes you have to find a safe place to put your bags and packs for a while, maybe an hour or two. Stores don't like to see things like that carried in. Shoplifting, you know."

Ryan nodded. "There were also a lot of cell phones charging. They're gone, too."

Dr. Sheila saw Connie steer her SUV into the parking lot. Ryan struggled to get up. He recognized the county logo on the door.

Dr. Sheila told him, "She's here to help."

As Connie parked the SUV, a young woman came out the front door, in a hurry to get to a parked car near the side. She looked to be in her 30s, with make-up and long hair, dressed nicely, definitely not a homeless person.

"Excuse me," Dr. Sheila said, getting up. "Can I talk to you?"

The woman barely slowed down.

"I have some questions." Dr. Sheila was persistent and moved to block the woman from her car. By then Connie had got out of her SUV and joined her.

"This ought to get interesting," Sid said in a low voice.

"Look, I have an appointment." The woman had her car

keys out.

"Do you work here?" Connie asked.

"I'm the assistant manager. I just started last week."

"Do you know what happened to this young man's — " Dr. Sheila pointed to Ryan " — backpack, maybe the other things, the cell phones?"

"We're tired of all that clutter." She was clearly angry. "People have got to understand they can't leave their filthy stuff here. It looks bad, who knows what's in them, probably attracts rats and mice. And electricity isn't free. These homeless people just can't use our electricity to charge their stupid cell phones."

Dr. Sheila held out her hands. "I understand, it has to be hard for you."

The woman was mollified, but only a little. "You have no idea, the things I've seen."

"I can only imagine. But can you tell me what happened to everything?"

The woman shrugged. "I tossed it all in the dumpster, in the back. Trash truck should be along soon to pick it all up."

Sid craned his neck around the corner of the building and spotted the large, green trash container. "Is there a lock on the lid?" he asked.

"Usually, but we take it off for trash day. Look, I have to go, I'm going to be late."

***

Connie and Sid walked over to the dumpster and raised the lid. He had to heft himself up a bit to see inside.

"The bags are still in here and there's a jumble of cell phones."

"Can you reach in?"

"Maybe, but…" he looked around and saw an empty crate near a door. "Get that and I'll stand on it."

One by one, Sid handed all of the packs and bags to Connie, who dropped them on the pavement in a pile.

"Not sure I'm getting all of the phones," he grunted, "they're pretty tangled up."

By now Ryan was able to stand up, and he had his few belongings by his side.

A couple of homeless men were coming down the sidewalk, and realized their packs were being taken from the dumpster. Connie told them what had happened. "I'm not sure you can leave your things here anymore."

They shook their heads, grabbed their packs, found their cell phones, and left. They knew they had no recourse, no options, and nothing to say.

***

Connie introduced herself to Sid. "Thanks for your

help." She saw his backpack frame and knew he was a transient, getting ready to hit the road.

"This is a beautiful dog," Dr. Sheila said, petting Ben. "He's a young dog, got a good coat on him. You're taking good care of him."

Sid walked over to his pack. He really wanted to be on his way, wasn't interested in any casual conversation about his dog.

Dr. Sheila said to Connie, "Ryan shouldn't be alone, at least for a while...he said he was camped at the gravel pit." She glanced at her watch. "I have a surgery in less than an hour."

"I'll take care of him," Connie assured her before turning to Ryan.

"You know Rex, right? We're friends." It was a stretch to say she and Rex were friends, but she had to get him to trust her. "I can take you to the camp. Somebody will be there in case you need help. It's a few miles, maybe you shouldn't walk that far."

Ryan was clearly reluctant.

Connie had an idea.

"Sid, can you and Ben come with us? We can drop Ryan off, and I'll drive you to the intersection with the south highway. You'll be able to pick up a ride to wherever you're going a lot easier, save you some time. We owe you that much for your help."

Sid thought for a moment. He knew the area she was talking about, and it would help him make up for lost time.

He also knew what the social worker was doing, enlisting his help because he was one of Ryan's "kind." He shrugged. "Sure."

It worked. Ryan accepted Connie's help.

Holding Classy, the boy sat in the front seat of the SUV. Sid motioned for Ben to jump in the back, then placed his backpack behind the seat, and climbed in.

Connie walked Dr. Sheila a few paces across the parking lot.

"Ryan's dog still has a rabies tag on his collar," Dr. Sheila said when they were out of earshot. "I have the number. I'll text it to you."

"Oh! I can trace it back to where his home might be."

Dr. Sheila turned to nod at the building. "Are all homeless shelters run this way?"

"No. I'll report this to my manager. We'll get with their board, do that inspection, and see what can be done. This was not acceptable."

Connie put a hand on Dr. Sheila's shoulder and chuckled. "I got to say, you really handled that little twit of an assistant manager quite well." Connie was sincere. "I might not have kept my temper."

Dr. Sheila smiled and turned to leave. "The last year of veterinary school, we all have to take Diplomacy 101. I got all A's!"

Connie laughed. The veterinarian was joking, right? *Right?*

She wasn't so sure.

CHAPTER TWENTY-ONE
CAN YOU STAY?

Connie made a quick phone call before pulling out of the parking lot. She steered the SUV into traffic and a few minutes later made a detour. She stopped in front of a pizza place.

"I'm betting you're hungry, my treat," she said, before exiting the vehicle and running into the shop. A minute later she emerged with three large boxes and two six packs of sodas. Sid opened the back door and she slid them in beside him on the seat. The aroma quickly filled the interior.

"That's a lot of pizza," Ryan remarked.

"There might be a few others at the camp, don't want to skimp for them," Connie answered.

But when they arrived, the camp was empty. Connie got out and called for Rex, but there was no answer. His dog was gone, too. Perhaps somebody else had stayed?

Ryan stepped out of the vehicle and let Classy go. Sid was next to get out, then Ben.

"Huh. Thought somebody might be here," Connie muttered, hands on hips.

"Probably be back in a few minutes," Ryan suggested. He really wanted the social worker to be gone. He was afraid she'd start to ask questions, and while he was grateful for her help, he did not want this day to be even worse than it was. He glanced at his tent. If his stepdad had reported it, and the other items, as stolen, Ryan would be in a lot of trouble.

The pizza boxes were placed on the table and opened.

Connie wasn't sure what to do. She had to get back to her office, there was an important meeting coming up and she couldn't miss it.

Sid was hungry, he'd only had an apple and oat bar for breakfast. He looked at the sun, it would be close to one o'clock by now. He could have been a hundred miles down the road by now. He took a slice of the pizza, thinking he and Ben would get back in the SUV. The social worker had said she'd take him to the intersection and he was determined to take her up on her offer.

It was clear she was worried.

"I can't leave you here alone, Ryan," she finally said. He tried to protest but she held up her hands. "If you have another episode, you'll need help. And if it's worse..." the words hung in the air.

Ryan was beginning to get frantic. He looked over at Sid. He had an idea. "Maybe he can stay with me?" he asked.

Sid held up his hands, but Connie said, "I don't know, we've already imposed on him enough. But please, perhaps you can stay? I have to get back to the office, and if he's alone, has another attack," she nodded to Ryan, "and can't get to his inhaler in time, well, I don't know..."

Sid was clearly reluctant.

"Look," Connie pleaded. "I'm going to call the health clinic this afternoon and arrange to pick up a better inhaler for him, a prescription, first thing in the morning. How about this. I'll drive you to the intersection. I'll even take you to wherever you want to go. New Mexico? Alabama? Vermont? Kentucky? I have some vacation time coming."

Sid chuckled at the absurd offer, and Connie smiled back. He liked the social worker, she had a good sense of humor. He took a deep breath.

"All right, I'll stay, just until morning." He looked around. As homeless camps go, this wasn't the worst he'd seen. *But*, it was still a homeless camp. He could stay here one night, but only one night.

Connie's phone chimed. She glanced down, saw the text from Dr. Sheila with Classy's tag number. That would be something else to do for Ryan tomorrow, track down the boy's family.

As she drove away, she was disappointed Rex wasn't there. She had decided to tell him about the Rippers, the rumors, to warn him and the others. But just as well, she thought. She didn't want them to panic and move into the larger camp, since it was going to be cleared out and bulldozed by the sheriff's office in the next few days. What good would telling him do?

***

"That's our bubble over there," Classy said to Ben.

"Bubble?"

"Yeah, where we sleep."

Ben tilted his head and looked at the object Classy had indicated with her nose.

"Uhm, they call it a tent."

Classy shrugged a little dog shrug. "It's a bubble, it's round and it just showed up one day on the ground. That means it can float away, too. Like a bubble."

Ben wasn't about to argue, but thought it was no wonder that Classy was sometimes called a "silly little terrier."

They wandered off, sniffing things and trotting towards the pond, Classy chatting the whole way about frogs and birds and small animals and big animals she had seen. "Some are kind of scary and they don't talk much, but others are my friends. But," she stopped and tilted her head, "I don't understand a thing they say."

Ben listened to her chatter. Maybe Classy wasn't silly as much as uncontrollably happy.

***

With Connie gone, Ryan felt a little more at ease. He finished one of the pizzas.

Some color was returning to the boy's face and he was breathing a little easier.

"That was a pretty bad attack," Ryan told Sid, looking down. He was still embarrassed.

"Do you get them often?" Sid asked.

"Not as often as I used to…when I was still at home." Ryan waved a hand. "Out here, things aren't as bad, don't have everybody yelling at me."

Sid opened a can of soda and took a long drink. He didn't want to ask the boy too many questions. He recognized that shyness, that reluctance to open up. Many years ago, that was him.

He changed the subject.

"That's a real cute dog you have over there."

"Classy? Yeah, she's my best bud, you wouldn't know she was almost ten years old, would you. My dad — my real dad — got her for me as a birthday present when I was six. Furry little puppy. She's smart, always seems to know what I want before I do. No way I'd leave her, she'll always be with me." Ryan shook his head "Don't want me, don't want my dog. That's what I told them when I left."

Sid did some quick math. Ryan had just told him he was only about sixteen. Too young to be out here.

He thought Ryan would stop talking, but the boy circled back to his past life. Sid took another pull from the soda can, sat back, and listened.

"I think I knew I was going to leave for a year, maybe more, before I finally did it," Ryan said, holding his hands on his lap, shoulders slumped. "My dad pretty much disappeared when I was twelve, didn't see much of him after that, and my mom got married to a guy who didn't like me from the start. Oh, he tried, I think to get to her, if you know what I mean. Took me to a baseball game, couple of movies. He's a big guy, with a big gut, really into watching those dumb wrestling shows on TV. Never did understand that.

"It got harder with him. Every time I had an asthma attack, he'd say I was faking it, just to get attention. My mom," he paused. "My mom tried to tell him how asthma works, how I can't breathe, but he wouldn't listen."

"Then she just gave up trying to explain. She gave up on me." Ryan paused, opened another can of soda.

"My grades got real bad, and I got into a fight, well, not a fight really, just another kid and I got to screaming at each other. You know, names and things. I had an attack, a bad one. Principal called my mom, she had to come get me and take me to the emergency room.

"My stepdad just lost it, said I was costing him a fortune, that emergency room bill was gonna be thousands, and who did I think I was anyway. He was yelling at me and I think he was set on hitting me. I grabbed Classy and ran outside, hid in a nearby field. She was shaking, scared out of her wits. So was I.

"That night, I left. Well," Ryan shrugged and smiled. "Not before I broke into the garage and took some things." He nodded at the tent. "Brand new, still in the box. And his sleeping bag, flashlight, camping gear, took those, too.

"That was a few months ago, been on my own ever since."

"Nobody's come looking for you?" Sid asked, but he knew the answer.

"Nah. My stepdad, my mom, they'd want that tent back. But they wouldn't want me."

They watched Classy and Ben near the pond, exploring like dogs do.

Ryan had an idea. "Hey, maybe I ought to be like you, hitting the road, hitchhiking from here to there." His smile was sudden, broad. "A real Road Warrior!"

Sid wasn't amused, and started to tell him that wasn't a good idea, when a man on a bicycle appeared. A hauler was hitched to it, bumping along with the ruts and holes in the road.

"There's Rex." Ryan said. They watched him dismount the bike. He unzipped the netting on the hauler and out bounded a dog. "And Brutus."

Ryan stood up and glanced at the pizza boxes. "At least we have a lot left for him."

**

Brutus stretched and shook himself. He liked going places with Rex, but the hauler was hard on his old bones and muscles. He padded over to the pond to lap up some water and saw Classy with Ben.

They immediately engaged in the obligatory sniffing and ear twitching that dogs do when they first meet.

"Is that your guy there?" Brutus asked Ben.

"Sid. He's a good guy. We've been through some things together." He didn't feel compelled to tell Brutus he and Sid had been together only a few days, it wasn't any of his business.

"Ben's a good guy, too," Classy said, tail wagging. He felt it was his responsibility to make sure the bigger dogs got along.

Brutus sat down and licked his paws. When a dog licked his paws, it meant everything was going to be OK.

"Brutus and Rex, they were here when Ryan and me showed up. Made things easy for us."

"Thanks for the compliment, Classy," Brutus nuzzled the little dog on her neck. "That's our home, over there," Brutus indicated the box near the clearing. "Been there a few years now. It's called a van."

"Do you like it here?" Ben asked, just making conversation.

Brutus got serious. "I think so. I don't remember much about past days. I forget a lot. Actually, I forget just about everything."

Classy stopped sniffing around a tree and looked at the two bigger dogs. "I remember everything about everything," she announced. "Maybe that's good, maybe not, but I sure wish I could forget some things. Maybe everything, like you, Brutus. Might make life easier."

Ben wanted to change the subject. It was nice talking to nice dogs, but he didn't want them to start asking him any questions. "Classy showed me the pond, you want to show me around the rest of the place?" he asked Brutus.

"Sure, a few things to see, some thistles you want to stay away from. Real sticky things." He glanced at Ben. "With that fur of yours, you'd be a mess in no time."

The three dogs set off.

***

Ryan told Rex what had happened at the homeless shelter.

"I've wondered about that place," Rex said, helping himself to a slice of pizza. "Some are saying the staff isn't too friendly."

"They're right," Ryan agreed.

Rex nodded to Sid. "Sorry I wasn't here. I had probably just left, missed you on the highway. Wanted to just stretch my legs a bit, try out my new bike. There's a nice trail on the other side. You staying here for a while?"

"Just until morning. I told that social worker I would, in case Ryan needs help." Sid pointed across the clearing. "I saw an old service road over there. That's where I'll pitch my tent."

"Nobody will bother you," Rex told him.

"He's a Road Warrior!" Ryan laughed. "Just like in those movies set in the future."

Rex's eyebrows shot up. "You're Rubber Trash?"

Sid smiled. "I prefer the old word. Hitcher. Don't want to be staying in one place too long. I like being on my own."

Sid picked up his backpack. Rex walked with him across the clearing.

"Thanks for helping the boy."

"I didn't do that much."

"Sounds to me like you did." Rex looked back at Ryan, who was helping himself to yet another slice of pizza.

"For such a scrawny kid, he sure eats a lot," Rex chuckled, then he shook his head, suddenly serious. "He really shouldn't be out here, not like this."

Sid nodded. "He told me a little about himself."

"Sad story, and nothing bad's happened to him. But," he looked knowingly at Sid, "just a matter of time…"

Sid nodded. He knew what Rex was talking about. Youngsters on the street, homeless, were easy prey to some of the worst monsters out there.

"I'm trying to talk him into getting help from one of the teen shelters. This town has a couple of good ones, but he doesn't want to hear that. Yet."

"Hopefully he will, sooner than later. Maybe I'll put in a word in the morning before I leave. Two of us saying the same thing might help."

Rex nodded. "I'll get him to stay with me in the van tonight. If he has another episode, I can get to him in time, make sure he has his inhaler. It's good he's got that social worker, Connie, looking out for him now."

"She seems to care."

Rex nodded. "She's better than others I've met, but she's only one person. Has limitations, you know. But she tries, more than most."

Sid turned to follow the service road, then told Rex, "Sounds to me like *you're* the one helping Ryan more than most."

***

The service road was overgrown with brush and grass, barely noticeable. Sid thought about leaving the tent rolled up, just using his sleeping bag, but with the pond over the way, there would be plenty of mosquitoes and gnats, especially at night.

He pitched the tent in a secluded spot under some low-hanging cottonwood branches, then wandered past the clearing to get Ben. He found the dog with his new friends near the pond's edge and watched them for a while, plopping around in the cold water, soaking their feet.

"Come on, Ben," he called at last.

Ben's obedience was instant, and the two walked back towards the service road.

By now other homeless men had returned. There was still some pizza left and Ryan was re-telling his story about the shelter. They nodded to Sid as he walked past. They knew he was "one of them" but "*not* one of them."

Ryan was already telling them Sid was a Road Warrior.

***

Sid found a log to sit on to watch the blue sky turn into dusk. There would be a full moon tonight; he looked forward to a quiet, peaceful evening.

Ben settled down next to Sid.

"More adventures, eh, boy?" Sid scratched the dog's head.

Music wafted from the camp. Sid supposed it might be from Rex's van. Subtle strands from a guitar, then a gravelly voice singing about mist-covered mountains, battles, wars, ruined suns, pain, and a time to die. A familiar song Sid hadn't heard for a long, long time. And one he hadn't missed.

CHAPTER TWENTY-TWO
FURY

Ryan sat on a bench with Classy. Earlier, he had watched Sid and Rex talking and, of course, knew they were talking about him. It seemed *everybody* was talking about him now. He knew he'd been found out, and even though he'd agreed to meet that social services lady in the morning, he was thinking about making other plans.

He drew Classy onto his lap and scratched behind her ears, bending close to whisper, "How about you and me, we hit the road, just like ol' Sid does? We'll get up before dawn, before anybody else, take the tent, and our stuff, and leave."

Nodding, he bit his lower lip, and did a quick mental calculation. He had almost six dollars, not a lot, but he'd work along the way. Didn't Sid mention that's what he did sometimes?

"Sid says he's going south," he muttered. "We'll go west. Maybe Nevada. Or California. Always wanted to see the ocean."

He stood up as Rex walked over to him.

"Hey, Ryan, why don't you sleep in the van tonight, I got room, just in case you need somebody. Is that OK?"

Ryan nodded and smiled. "Great idea, I'll get my sleeping bag."

He wasn't about to tell Rex his plans.

***

Ben watched Sid crawl into the tent, then followed him. The netting was zipped up and the small light came on. He crouched down, but kept his head up, looking outside.

"Keeping first watch?" he heard Sid ask, chuckling, ruffling up the fur on his head, scratching behind his ears. He still didn't know what that meant but it always made Sid smile.

I wonder if Classy and Brutus are still in the water? Ben wondered. He would have liked to have stayed outside a little longer, it was nice to have nice dogs to talk to.

***

It was warm in the tent. Sid took off his shirt and shoes, but left his pants on. His money belt stuck to his skin, but he'd take that off later. He was only staying the night, no reason to hide it. By the glow of the small flashlight, he reached for his book and began to read.

One of the camp dogs began to bark.

***

Ben stood up, and pawed at the zippered opening.

"What?" Sid asked. "Come on, boy, lay down. Those dogs probably just barking at a raccoon or something."

Sid heard a truck roar into the clearing, its horn insisting on attention. Doors slammed, men shouted.

Laughter, loud and mean. The kind of laughter you never hear from a homeless camp.

Ben was frantic.

Sid unzipped the tent to get a better look. Ben bolted out, running as fast as he could toward the camp.

"Ben!" The dog paid Sid no mind.

Shirtless, Sid scrambled after him. *Now* what could this dog possibly be running after???

***

Brutus ran out of the van, Classy right behind him. "Something's not right," Brutus panted. "*Somebody's* not right."

***

Rex followed the dogs. What he saw outside almost made him laugh. Three men were wearing ridiculous masks, Halloween-like, comical. Then he realized there was nothing funny about them. They were carrying large knives and were coming towards him.

"Come out, you worthless pieces of trash!" the man in the monkey face mask yelled. He was a tall man, and spun around in circles, yelling and brandishing a knife. "We're not going to hurt you."

He turned over tables, picked up chairs to send them flying. "You're not welcome in this town."

A man wearing a clown face was placing tubes holding fireworks on the ground, setting them on fire with a lighter. Another man, this one wearing a fox mask, ran past the van, looking for more tents to slash.

There was a loud bang and whoosh. Sid watched a trail of smoke erupt from the ground, pointing towards the trees. For some absurd reason, the music about wars and ruined suns was still blaring.

***

The camp's men scrambled out of tents and shelters, some tripping in their panic. Sid shouted to them, helped some of them up.

"Get to the ponds and hide!" he yelled, running after them.

One of them was screaming into his cell phone. "They've got knives, they're gonna hurt us." But would anybody come? Would anybody care?

Sid looked for anybody else to help escape. Where was Rex? Where was Ryan? *Where was Ben???*

***

Rex ran towards the pond, calling for Brutus. He figured his dog would follow him. He had a brief thought about Sid, but his tent was far enough away, maybe he would stay put, unnoticed, and uninvolved.

He turned around. He didn't see Brutus, but saw Ryan.

***

Ryan was trying to grab Classy. She was barking incessantly, running back and forth from the van to the attackers, too fast for him to grab.

But somebody else did.

***

"We got us a little froo froo doggy!" Clown Face held Classy up by the scruff of her neck, wriggling to get free.

She managed a strangled, "Yip."

"Please, let her go," Ryan begged, trying to grab her. He stumbled to his knees. He looked up. "Please. She's just a little dog, won't hurt you. She's all I have."

Clown Face turned Classy this way and that, a sickening grin spreading across his face. "You want her? Sure, here you go," and Classy was hurled, nose over tail, past Ryan's head. "No!" he screamed, reaching for her, but it was too late. She landed with a sickening thud in the dirt several feet away.

Ryan felt his chest cave in as his lungs struggled for air.

The camp began to fill with smoke.

***

Ben saw Classy thrown to the dirt just as he came into the clearing. Brutus was barking, unsure what to do. He had never hurt a human in his life.

Ben hadn't, either. Until now.

He launched himself at the attacker, grabbing hold of his arm, hearing bones crunch, the man screeching in pain. Ben tasted blood.

***

There was another "Bang!" Another whoosh into the trees. Branches and leaves exploded in flames.

Sid called for Ben. Surely he wasn't in the camp, he must be with Rex and Ryan and their dogs, safe. Somewhere.

Seconds later, he heard high-pitched screams, and saw all of them in a horror scape. Time froze.

Here was Ben, his jaws in a death grip around a man's arm.

Then he saw Ryan.

The boy was laying on the ground, crying, gulping hard, his eyes bulging.

Rex was at the boy's side, trying to get him up. "Come on, we gotta get you out of here."

He bent down to lift Ryan, but his shoulder was grabbed, forcing him to drop the boy.

He turned around to see one of the raiders. Monkey Face laughed. "Where you going? We're just getting started."

Rex punched Monkey Face in the stomach. But Rex wasn't a fighter, the blow was soft, and Monkey Face hit Rex in the face, then wrenched his arm hard and away. Rex gasped from the pain, gripped his wrist, and collapsed on his knees. Monkey Face drew a leg back to kick Rex in his stomach.

***

Ben's jaws clenched around Clown Face's arm, not letting go. The dog's teeth gnawed and thrashed into flesh. The man was doing all he could to shake Ben off, but with each jerk, more blood spewed up in the air.

"Get him off, get him off!" His high-pitched shrieks pierced the air. Brutus was still barking, dodging back and forth towards Clown Face's legs.

***

Sid knew what he had to do. He plowed into Monkey Face, hitting him with all of the strength he had, knocking him to the ground. Spinning, he covered the distance to Ben in seconds, and began to pull at the dog's rear legs.

"Ben, let go, you've done your job," he gasped, trying to get the dog to open his jaws, let Clown Face go.

But Sid's arm was ruthlessly grabbed and he was spun around.

It was Monkey Face. Sid saw he was holding a knife.

***

Ben would not let go. All of the happiness and love he had found with Sid was gone now, replaced by a furious revenge against the person who had let him down. The person who had abandoned him on that hot and dusty road. He wanted to hurt that person, like he had been hurt.

That person wasn't here, but this one would do very nicely.

In his fury, he did not notice, and did not care, that black smoke was billowing out of the van.

***

Rex saw several more flames ignite in the dry leaves and brush. He knew his van was on fire. He had a propane gas tank inside, it was small but nearly full. They had to get out of there. The trees glowed, illuminating the night, but smoke made it difficult to see. His arm was broken and his stomach clenched with pain.

He couldn't get up.

***

No matter how hard he tried, Ryan couldn't catch his breath. His inhaler was in the van, but what good would it do with all of this smoke? He looked for Classy, saw her body in the dirt. He struggled to crawl to where she lay, mouthing her name, but failed to get the words out.

He reached her, she raised her little head and looked at him, the familiar look of love she had given him for so many years.

The last thing Ryan did before he died was to reach out and touch her.

***

Get up, Ryan, Classy told him. *You're always all right after one of these things, where's that tube you breathe into? Come on, Ryan.*

But Ryan lay still. This time was different. She was alone, now. There was nothing left for her to do, nothing left for her to live for. She coughed up some blood, then lay still.

Classy became what she had always wanted, a one-hundred-percent forgettin' kind of dog.

***

Rex watched them die. There was nothing he could do. He held his broken arm and sobbed.

***

Sid began to hammer at Monkey Face's head and shoulders. Monkey Face turned away but held onto the knife.

A large branch, engulfed in flames, came crashing down only a few feet away. It was enough of a distraction for Sid, who flinched. And that was enough for Monkey Face to get an advantage. His knife came down on Sid's face, carving a gash from his left eye to his lips.

"Aaahhh," Sid groaned, struggling to clear his mind from the pain. Blood ran down his neck onto his chest. He was close to blacking out.

Monkey Face saw the money belt and snatched it, ripping

it away from Sid's skin.

"What do we have here?" He could see the bills through the transparent vinyl. "Homeless trash ain't supposed to have money." His laugh was hysterical, mindless, as he waved it around.

Then he got a better look at Sid, kneeling in the dirt, holding his bloody face. "Bonus time, we not only got us a homeless dude, he's a —"

Sid's mind cleared and he saw his chance. With short jabs, he attacked the man's face, his nose, his jaw, a familiar, satisfying feeling as bone splintered. Blood spluttered out, covering the man's shirt. The money belt flew out of Monkey Face's hand, landing in flames.

Sid didn't stop. He bent down to pick up a rock and smashed it into Monkey Face's temple, forcing him to bend over. Sid used his right knee and brought it up hard into the man's chin.

Sid had some built-up fury, too.

"Finish the job! Finish the job!" Sid screamed, a mindless mantra erupting out of his past. He felt no pain from his wounds, he was out of control now, and he knew it.

***

Monkey Face was in bad shape, but somehow, he held onto his knife. He drew it back, ready to thrust it into Sid's chest.

***

Out of the corner of his eye, Ben saw Monkey Face holding a knife.

With a rip of flesh, Ben hurled himself away from Clown Face's arm.

The dog leaped and his huge body smashed into Monkey Face's shoulder, knocking him off balance. The knife fell to the dirt.

Monkey Face began to fall, the dog still on him, when the night turned red and black and red again. The van seemed to disappear in a gut-wrenching, ear-splitting explosion. Debris hit the trees, then fell in a dangerous cascade of rusty and jagged metal.

Ben had no control over his body. He felt himself lifted into the air, his legs flailing. He landed hard on rocks, a loud "Whoof" coming from his lungs. He struggled to get back up. He coughed, the smoke was heavy and he could smell his fur, singed from the fire.

The dog felt the ground shake again, the air was sucked out of his lungs. He looked up. And saw himself falling, falling, falling.

***

Fox Face had found only a couple of tents and canvas awnings on the south side some distance from the clearing. He did what they came for, ripping and cutting the fabric with his knife. It got hung up in some thin twine and he had to shake it free, and was heading back to the camp when the van exploded.

"What the —" he muttered. He began to run back to the camp. He covered his head with his arms to protect it against the onslaught of burning branches raining down.

What he saw in the clearing was something out of a movie, people laying on the ground, blood everywhere, the ground smothered by debris, metal, wood, and what was left of the van. Monkey Mask was on his knees, Clown Face was crying, holding on to an arm, or what was left of it. He had been gone only a minute, maybe two!

Fox Face panicked, ran towards the truck, but turned back. He had to help his friends, didn't he? Somehow, he urged Clown Face to get moving, then got Monkey Face into the cab. By now most of the trees around the camp were on fire.

"Gotta get outta here. Get you guys help. This has gone all wrong, all wrong. The cops are coming, can't you hear the sirens?"

He started the motor, the truck's wheels spun in the soft dirt as he backed up and gunned it. They raced away towards the highway.

***

Sid couldn't hear anything, the explosion had deafened him. He figured it had done the same with the others. He shook his head to clear it, sending blood flying. His face spasmed with pain. He couldn't get up off the ground, not even to his knees.

Where was Ben?

Sid shook his head again. He needed to stay awake. The smoke was getting heavier.

Several feet away, he saw Ben struggling to stand up.

***

Ben couldn't seem to find the ground. He was panting heavily, he knew he had to move, but his brain was addled, confused. The smoke lifted just a bit, and he saw Sid laying on the ground. Their eyes met.

***

Sid saw amber eyes.

***

Ben saw dark brown eyes.

***

What was left of the van shook and screeched. In less than a heartbeat, the walls twisted and collapsed on top of Ben in a torrent of dirt and ash.

***

Ben disappeared as Sid felt his own heart sink down into the deepest part of his soul.

Before he lost consciousness, his last thought was: "I love you, Good Boy Ben."

CHAPTER TWENTY-THREE
WHERE'S BEN?

D r. Sheila locked the front door of the veterinary hospital and joined her husband at his truck. Both were ready to go home.

"Didn't they warn us about late night emergency operations in vet school?" she asked him, rubbing her neck.

"They did, but we ignored it or maybe we cut class that day. Remember, we were going to run a tight ship, forty-hour weeks, closed on weekends," Dr. Jim answered. They laughed.

Dr. Jim started the truck and steered it onto the busy highway. He was about to turn, when Dr. Sheila grabbed his arm. She pointed to the south. The sky was glowing.

"There's a fire. Look at all that smoke." Her eyes grew wide. "Oh, no, I think I know where it's coming from. Jim, go the other way, hurry."

***

Connie was just leaving another meeting of the city council. It had gone late, with debate, discussion, and arguments, about Sheriff Stewart's plans to clean out the large homeless camp. Connie was glad to see that not everyone agreed it was a good idea.

Her cell chimed. Emergency dispatch told her something had happened at the gravel pits. Fire engines and an ambulance were on route.

"I'll be there in ten minutes."

***

Sirens blaring, Sheriff Stewart pulled his police car up beside the fire truck. "What a mess," he muttered to himself, got out and stepped into muck. The stench was almost over-powering. Trees were still smoldering, the cause of most of the smoke. Pieces of tents and canopies lay about in the dirt. Pots, pans, bottles, broken boxes, and crates were strewn about.

Headlights from all of the emergency vehicles helped to provide lighting but it was difficult to make his way, having to step over the debris.

"A propane tank in an old van exploded." The fire marshal came up to him. He waved a hand around the scene. "We found evidence of fireworks. They're what started the fires."

Three ambulances were on the other side of the clearing, several men whom the sheriff assumed were some of the homeless campers, were standing next to it. As he got closer, he saw Connie. She had beat him to the scene.

"We have one fatality," Connie told him, clearly upset. "Ryan. Only a boy. A teenager."

He looked around. "The guys who did this, they're gone?"

She nodded.

The headlights of another truck appeared down the road and pulled over into some brush. Connie motioned to Dr. Sheila and Dr. Jim as they got out and joined her at one of the ambulances.

"What happened?" Dr. Sheila asked.

"They were attacked," Connie answered. "Men with knives. Rippers." She choked back her tears. "Rex got hurt, not too bad, his wrist's broken and he has lots of scrapes. But Sid got cut really bad, his face. Lost a lot of blood. Ambulances took both of them to the hospital."

She motioned to the homeless men standing near the fire truck. "They're saying Sid risked his life to help them, saved Rex's life."

"But Ryan." Connie bit her lip. She wiped away tears on her cheeks. "He didn't make it. He's over there, they covered his body."

"The boy. Oh, no." Dr. Sheila walked the few feet to where Ryan was, and bent down to touch the sheet. She could feel her own tears begin.

Then she saw the short tail, fur matted with dirt and death, just to the side. "Oh, Classy," she moaned, reaching over to pick up the lifeless little body. It sagged in her arms.

Dr. Jim joined her, kneeling. "Put her with him," he suggested, lifting the sheet up just enough for her to slide the little dog next to Ryan's body.

"Sleep your peace forever, little Classy," she whispered.

The lump in her throat was making it difficult for her to speak. She stood up, looked around, and had the clarity of mind to ask:

"Where's Ben?"

***

Connie asked the homeless men if they had seen Sid's dog.

One of them had Brutus on a leash, the stout dog seemed no worse for the wear from the night's mayhem. "I know Brutus was close to him at one point," he told them.

"A guy in a mask had Classy by the scruff of his neck, then threw him on the ground. Ben attacked the guy, latched on to him, had a good grip on his arm. Pretty sure he did some damage, it was hard to tell how much with all of the smoke." He shook his head. "That dog would not let go. Until," he paused, "he saw the other guy attack Sid, then Ben went after that guy, too. It all happened so fast."

Dr. Jim got a flashlight from his truck. Connie joined the two veterinarians and some of the homeless men in the search, looking behind the ruins of the van, in the brush and weeds near the pond, calling his name.

They were about to give up. Even with the fires extinguished, the air was still smoky. Connie said she wanted to get to the hospital to see how Sid was doing, when Brutus began to whine, straining against his leash. The man holding him let go, and the dog made a beeline toward a large piece of sheet metal laying on the ground.

It had a suspicious lean to it.

"Over here!" Connie shouted.

***

Twp of the homeless men picked up the metal. Underneath was a sickening sight. Ben lay in a heap of matted fur.

Dr. Jim felt for a pulse. "He's alive, but just barely."

They checked for obvious wounds. "I can't see much," Dr. Sheila said, "he's covered with dirt and ash."

"His breathing is shallow." Dr. Jim shook his head. "Let's get him to our hospital."

Ben was carefully rolled onto a piece of flat wood, then carried to the bed of Dr. Jim's truck. Dr. Sheila climbed in to cushion the dog's head against the jolts on the road.

CHAPTER TWENTY-FOUR
THE STILL-STRONG HEARTS

Their busy day had already led them to near-exhaustion just an hour ago. But the two veterinarians rallied their bodies and minds to do what they could for Ben.

They brought the unconscious dog into the surgery on a wheeled gurney and gently lifted him onto the operating table.

"I don't see any blood," Dr. Sheila muttered, dislodging pieces of dirt and gravel. She began to clean the matted fur as well as she could with warm water and a sponge. "His fur is singed in spots, but fortunately his skin didn't get burned."

Dr. Jim held a stethoscope to Ben's chest. "I don't like the way his lungs sound, they might be damaged from all that smoke."

Working quickly, they cleaned off his mouth, nose, and eyes. "No injuries to his face," Dr. Sheila said. They moved down to his legs. "Oh, no. This front leg is badly swollen."

"Let's get him into X-ray."

A few minutes later, they were inspecting the scan.

Dr. Jim shook his head. "The bones are completely crushed. This leg took the full force of the metal falling on him."

There were only two things that could be done: Put Ben down, or amputate the leg. Amputation was risky. Would Ben's heart hold out? But how could they proceed without the owner's permission, and the owner was Sid, in the hospital, himself in bad shape?

"I'll call Connie."

Dr. Sheila quickly explained the situation. "We're looking for guidance. There's no guarantee Ben will make it, but we have to make a decision now."

"I'm at the hospital. Sid's in surgery, they're trying to save his eye," Connie explained. "They did an MRI and he has a serious concussion." She thought for a second. "I'll go ahead and authorize the operation. I'll find the money for it somehow."

Without hesitating, Dr. Sheila responded, "No, Connie, don't worry about that. There won't be a bill from us. We just needed your permission."

***

Ben was put on an I.V., hooked up to the heart monitor, then given an anesthesia. Working together, they shaved the fur around the chest and the upper part of the leg, exposing the skin. After a thorough cleaning, they were ready.

"You do this," her husband told her. "You're better than I am."

Dr. Sheila's scalpel cut into the dog's chest in one efficient, smooth movement. Dr. Jim stanched blood and tied off blood vessels. He kept a close eye on the heart monitor while Dr. Sheila exposed the shoulder bone, careful not to damage muscle and tissue.

Since the front leg was being amputated, the shoulder joint was fairly easy to dislodge. A minute later, Dr. Jim took the leg away; the process of suturing the large incision began.

The whole operation had taken less than an hour.

"Nice job," Dr. Jim said. He was cleaning the table as his wife finished the sutures.

"Thanks," she took a big sigh, then stepped back. "I can't count how many times I've amputated legs. Almost all of them do really well on three legs but it's never an easy decision."

"His heart is holding on." Dr. Jim looked at the monitor. "At least he's got that going for him."

Dr. Sheila stroked Ben's head, a softness in her eyes. "You're such a good boy," she whispered. "You've STILL got a strong heart, keep it going for us — and Sid — will you?"

***

The surgeon found Connie in the waiting room at the hospital. Since Sid had no known relatives (certainly none in the area, and just as important none who could be found, and even more important, none that might care), Connie had signed all of the paperwork the hospital asked for, but she couldn't even tell them his last name. By default, she was Sid's primary contact.

"He's still unconscious. He has a bad concussion so we'll do another MRI tomorrow and monitor it. We think we saved his eye," the surgeon told her, "but the knife nicked the retina. He will probably have some vision challenges. We'll bring in an ophthalmologist for a consult.

"The wound to his face, that's another matter. It's pretty deep. He might have nerve damage in his cheek. He also has a couple of cracked ribs. He's going to be pretty stiff and sore for a while."

He looked down at his notes. "He has an interesting scar on his lower back. An old one." He shrugged. "It might be a bullet wound."

She raised her eyebrows. Perhaps Sid had been in trouble when he was younger. Gangs? Did he have a rap sheet? She would probably never know.

"When will he wake up?" she asked.

"Maybe tomorrow. We want his brain to rest as much as possible, and he'll be on pain medication."

Connie nodded. "I appreciate all you're doing for him."

"I hear he's kind of a hero, maybe helped save some people?"

"Yes. He did."

"It's fortunate he's in pretty good shape, his lungs are excellent and his heart is still strong."

***

Connie needed to get home, to bed. This had been one of the longest nights in her life. She would text the office and let them know she was taking the day off. Sleeping until noon was her only plan.

She saw a familiar face coming down the hall. Pastor Larry reached her, shaking his head.

"I am so sorry I didn't get up here before now," he said. "I got volunteers and two busses to pick up those poor men and whatever belongings we could salvage from their camp."

"You've had your hands full. Where are they now?" she asked.

"We have them – and their dogs – in a couple of churches, their meetings halls and community buildings. They're safe and they can stay there as long as they need to."

They sat down in a common area that had several stuffed chairs and small tables.

He told her Rex was downstairs, being tended to. "Nothing major, fortunately, a broken wrist, lots of bruises. He said some guy, Sid, and his dog, Ben, saved him and a lot of the others."

He hadn't met Sid, she told him what she knew about the hitch hiker. "He was just passing through, and this happened to him," she leaned back in the chair, shaking her head. "And that's on me. I asked him to stay."

Pastor Larry tilted his head. "It sounds like it was a good thing he was there this night…" he began.

"Not without cost," she interrupted, "and his dog is losing a leg even as we speak." She went to pick up her bag; a large envelope a nurse had given her poked out of the top. It held everything that had been in Sid's pants pockets, which wasn't much.

"You can be my witness when I look at this," she muttered. She spilled the contents out on a table.

Almost ninety dollars and some change.

A wadded-up receipt from a local taco shop.

An old leather wallet, not in the best of shape. It was almost empty inside, except for two items: A Social Security card with Sid's full name (at least now she could tell the hospital) and the other a business card for an organic grocery store in another state.

She handed the wallet to Pastor Larry. He turned it over and looked up at her.

"Do you know what this means?" he asked her, pointing out some embossed letters on the leather.

She shook her head. He took the wallet back and read the letters to her:

U.S.M.C.

She shrugged, still not understanding what this meant.

When Pastor Larry told her, she knew she wouldn't be taking the next day off.

CHAPTER TWENTY-FIVE
FOUR

The headlines on the front page of the morning newspaper screamed:

ATTACK ON HOMELESS CAMP
LEAVES ONE DEAD, CARNAGE

The sub headlines began to tell the story:

Many Injured.
Fire destroys campsite.
Sheriff reports homeless fought back "courageously"
Local vigilantes ruthless.

One in hospital in serious condition,
might lose an eye

Dog saved owner

ARREST WARRANTS ISSUED FOR THREE

FOURTH SUSPECT WITH KNOWLEDGE OF
ATTACK SOUGHT
COMMUNITY FUND SET UP TO
HELP THE VICTIMS

***

Connie did not take the day off.

Just before eight o'clock in the morning, she was at her desk. She hoped she would need to make only one phone call. She was not in the mood to be put on hold, or given the run-around.

For some years, politicians and the United States Veteran's Administration have become aware that too many veterans are homeless, for any number of reasons. The response — and funding — has been quick and efficient, even though not as thorough as some believe it should be.

Veterans' housing is designated in many communities. Special teams make certain any and all benefits are received: Food, clothing, health care, counseling, and more.

Still, there are many veterans who remain "out there," unrecognized and lost, perhaps unwilling to come in for help. Eight percent? Ten percent? Twelve percent? Nobody knows, but there are veterans working hard to find them, veterans who care.

One of them was the person Connie called this morning. They had worked together a few times, helping homeless veterans with a variety of needs.

The team leader of the V.A. in the state answered on the second ring. Connie explained what had happened the previous night, and how Sid had risked his life, with considerable cost to him.

He took down the information she gave, assuring her that although it wasn't much, it was enough for him to work on.

"It's possible the wallet doesn't mean anything," he warned her. "He could have picked it up from a second-hand store, but I'll have an answer shortly. At least we have his last name and social security number. I'll email you what I find out."

Connie hung up and leaned back in her chair. She stared up at the ceiling. The V.A. officer was probably right, the wallet meant nothing. That meant she still had Sid and Ben on her hands. She felt very alone with those problems.

And hour later her computer chimed with incoming emails, and her phone rang.

"I sent you some files, but I thought I should talk to you," the V.A. officer told her. "I'm sending a resource leader. She'll get there tomorrow. When you read the email, you'll know why." He paused.

"We've been looking for this guy for quite a while."

***

Connie got a text message from Dr. Sheila.

Ben came through the surgery, we're letting him sleep for now, don't want him moving around too much for a few hours. Watching for infection.

She responded with a quick, *Got it, thanks, keep me updated. I'll be at the hospital later this morning. I'll let you know how Sid's doing.*

Connie printed out the documents from her emails, more than twenty pages to read and try to make sense of. As she organized them on her desk, she shook her head, then decided to make another call, this time to Sheriff Stewart. She wanted any information he had on last night's attack, and she also wanted him to know what she was learning about Sid. They agreed to meet at the hospital.

***

The doctor was coming out of Sid's room. "He's beginning to wake up, pretty groggy right now."

"We don't want to stress him out." Connie was carrying several folders in her arms. "We just have a few questions. An officer from the V.A. will be coming in. I'm sure she'll want to talk to you before she sees him."

"This guy's a veteran?"

Connie and the sheriff exchanged glances. "Yes. We've just found that out."

A minute later the nurse motioned them in. "He's more lucid, but if he begins to get tired…"

"We'll leave," Connie promised.

They found Sid propped up in his bed. He was dressed in a white hospital shift, a blanket pulled up to his chest. An I.V. led down to his right arm and a thin oxygen tube was in his nose. Half of his face, including his left eye, was covered in gauze, held in place by bands of tape. The color of the other half of his face was sallow. He looked up as Connie came in.

He held up a hand, a weak gesture of greeting. Connie introduced Sheriff Stewart to him.

She pulled a chair to one side of his bed, the sheriff did the same next to her.

"Sid, I know you're in pain, the doctor says you're groggy from all of the meds. We just want to talk to you for a few minutes, if you don't mind," she said, not entirely certain how to begin.

"How to begin" was taken out of her hands when Sid whispered one word: "Ben."

She leaned back in the chair. "He's going to be OK. He's at Dr. Sheila's veterinary hospital. They had to operate on him…"

His one good eye began to gleam and he shook his head slightly. "No. He's gone. I saw him get crushed."

Sheriff Stewart shook his head. "We found him, buried under a piece of metal, still alive."

"But," Connie added, "they had to amputate one of his legs. They couldn't save it." She hated telling him the truth, but it was best he knew now, not later.

Sid looked away, bit his lip, and swallowed hard. "Such a good boy," his words barely audible. They gave him a minute to think about what he had just been told.

He coughed. "What about Rex and the others?"

"Rex is OK, his arm is in a cast and he has a lot of bruises," Connie answered. "Some of the others were scuffed up a bit, but nothing major. They're staying in area churches. We'll find housing for them, they'll be taken care of. And their dogs, too. But..." her tone changed.

Sid knew he was about to get bad news.

Connie swallowed hard. "Ryan didn't make it. The coroner thinks the smoke, the stress from everything he was seeing, gave him an asthma attack that he couldn't survive. He couldn't breathe." She closed her eyes and bent her head down. "I am so sorry."

"Classy, his dog? I want to know."

"She's gone, too."

"Oh, no." Sid was clearly moved. "He would never leave her. She would never leave him."

Connie took a deep breath and continued. "We traced Classy's tags to Ryan's family, told his mother what happened to him. She's coming to get his body this week."

"And the stepdad?"

"Didn't mention him. Got the feeling he's no longer in the picture."

They shared a long gaze. They also shared a common, unspoken guilt. Connie, because she hadn't traced the tags the day before; Sid, because he should have talked Ryan into leaving the camp, take Classy, and go to a teen shelter.

"We didn't do very good by them, did we?" Sid groaned.

Sheriff Stewart cleared his throat, breaking the uncomfortable silence. "We got the goons who attacked you, all three of them. Two of them were hurt pretty bad. They're not too smart. Showed up in the emergency room downstairs. Of course, we had alerts out. The District Attorney is considering bringing murder charges. They'll be going away for a long time. We're looking for a fourth guy, he wasn't there but he knew about it. He'll face some accessory charges."

The sheriff leaned forward in his chair. "You got in some pretty good licks. The guy you wrangled with has a broken jaw. He's going to be eating his meals through a straw for the next few months."

"Just got some lucky punches in," Sid said. "They really didn't know what they were doing, not very good at fighting."

"That's an understatement. The one who drove them to the hospital was pretty chatty when we talked to him. He said they knew that homeless people don't have weapons. Figured they'd just cut up some tents, destroy whatever they could find. 'Run 'em out of town' was what he said. Didn't count on you putting up a fight. Or your dog. And," he chuckled, "you're going to love this. They had one of those dash cams on the truck, running the whole time. They were going to put it on the Internet, one of those chat groups, to show how brave they were."

Sid did find that amusing. "Great evidence."

"Yeah, the best kind. It's intense, shows what you did, what Ben did, going after the guy in the Clown Mask. That guy's going to need a lot of operations. His arm is mangled really bad."

"Ben's a hero," Connie added. "So are you. You saved Rex, helped some of the others, too."

Sid shook his head. "I didn't save everybody."

They knew he was talking about Ryan.

Connie opened one of the folders. She had to change the subject before she began to cry.

"But you've done good by lots of people, Sid, according to this."

She handed him a piece of paper. The Marine Corps logo was at the top.

"I saw your wallet, the one embossed with U.S.M.C. I made a call."

Sid barely glanced at the document before shoving it back to her. "You shouldn't have done that. That old wallet, I just got it out of some trash years ago."

"We know that's not true." His anger surprised her. She

opened up one of the other folders.

"Says here you were in a gunfight in the Middle East twenty years ago. You got fifteen of your fellow soldiers to safety, even carrying a wounded man to a medivac unit." She looked up. "You got wounded yourself. You were awarded the Purple Heart. Nominated for the Silver Star, and other medals. Only three men were lost, Sid." She looked back up at him. He didn't seem to be paying attention.

"Only three," she repeated.

He shook his head. "Four."

Connie glanced at the page again, showing it to the sheriff for confirmation, who nodded. "It says right here, three."

His next two words tore into her heart.

"Four. Ryan."

He turned over in the bed, away from them. The interview was over.

CHAPTER TWENTY-SIX
BONDS

I'm worried about Ben." Dr. Sheila looked up at her husband when he came into the boarding annex. She was sitting on the floor in one of the large cages, stroking the dog's head. An I.V. line stretched to the cage's top, giving Ben liquid nourishment.

It had been almost twelve hours since his surgery, his temperature normal, and his heart was beating stronger. But he hadn't regained consciousness.

"We could give him a reversal to the anesthesia, but let's wait a bit longer." He leaned against the cage's door. "We don't want him moving around too much."

She stood up. "I was just hoping there'd be some sign of waking up, awareness."

***

Ben *was* aware. Sort of. He heard unfamiliar voices and his name a few times, but none of it made sense.

He was in a blackness that was blacker than black, not standing or sitting or walking or running. Looking around, he couldn't see anything or anyone, just more blackness.

Thinking was hard, remembering even harder. *Come on,*

he said to himself, *you're a half-remembering kind of dog, remember?* He laughed out loud. *I can't be too bad off if I can make a joke.*

He closed his eyes, needing to get his bearings.

His ball. Running after his ball. Waiting, waiting, waiting on a road. Hot. Thirsty. Hungry. The Baybee. Treats. Getting into cars. Getting out of cars. Walking on a trail, filled with scents he had never smelled before. Sleeping in a balloon. Wait, no that's not what it was called, but what was it?

And Sid. Where was Sid?

Shouting, anger, so much anger. Blood in his mouth. The smell of smoke. Loud sounds. Dirt. Pain.

Oh! There's Sid. One last memory. Sid laying on the ground, not moving.

What happened?

His heart hurt. He had tried to help, at least he thought he had. Had he done something wrong — again?

He wasn't a good boy, was he. No, everything he did was wrong. And now he was alone.

Yes, Ben *was* aware. But why? What was the use anymore? He edged back into blackness.

***

Dr. Sheila texted Connie later that day, asking her to stop by the vet hospital.

"You look exhausted," she said to Dr. Sheila. They were sitting in her office sipping tea, both women trying to relax.

"You don't look a whole lot better yourself," came the good-natured retort. They both laughed.

Connie shook her head. "I can't believe this last twenty-four hours. I feel shell shocked."

"How's Sid?"

"Not good. Depressed. He blames himself for what happened to Ben and to Ryan, even Classy. He shouldn't, it's those goons who attacked the camp..." Her voice faltered as she took another sip of the tea. "I hope those so-called Rippers get everything that's coming to them."

Dr. Sheila nodded. "Maybe this will help." She slid several envelopes across the desk. "People have been stopping by, they read the paper and want to help."

Connie reached over to the envelopes, leafing through them, then looked up in shock. "There's money in them!"

"We have more than three thousand dollars. And people are calling, asking what they can do. What happened to Ben, and Sid, has really touched them."

"This is extraordinary. You have the surgery costs covered."

"Oh, no," Dr. Sheila held up her hands. "I said no charge and I meant it. This will go to Sid. We'll set up a bank account for him. He'll have a lot of hospital bills."

Connie leaned back in her chair. "Maybe he won't. Let

me tell you a story about Sid. It's a good thing you're sitting down."

***

Sid was wheeled through the hospital aisles to get another MRI. His head hurt and he'd only been able to drink water.

He was told to lay still while the machine did its job, showing the technicians sitting on the other side of the glass the inside of his brain. He knew the concussion was bad, he'd had them before. Many times.

He thought about Ben. Because of him, Ben was now an amputee, a dog with only three legs. How good would that be for the big dog? What kind of life would he have now? What had he been thinking, taking him on the road, maybe he'd been better off in the shelter. He could have found a good home for himself.

I failed him.

His mind turned to Ryan. That poor kid, never had a chance. Why didn't he talk to him more, get him help? Yeah, he was going to do it the next day, but why did he wait?

I failed him, too.

Even the thought of Classy punched his heart. Spunky little fluff of fur, always at Ryan's side. He knew how much the dog meant to the boy. His words came back to him like a hammer: "Don't want me, don't want Classy."

I have failed everybody and everything that has come my way. The choices I've made have come at a terrible cost.

I cannot touch anything without cost.

***

"I don't know." Dr. Jim took his stethoscope away from Ben's chest and put it in his lab pocket. "He should be awake by now." It was now eighteen hours since the operation. Dr. Sheila and an assistant were changing out the dog's bedding and I.V. bottle.

"Let's back off of the pain medication a little?" she suggested.

"I'll do that if he doesn't wake up tomorrow morning. We need to get something solid in his belly."

Dr. Sheila bent down to the prone dog, ruffling his ears, hoping to get a response. She was unrewarded. "I hope he hasn't given up, he has so much to live for. But," she remembered what Connie had told her, "Sid's the same way. Not doing good at all. Those two have such an incredible bond."

They closed the cage's door and went out into the lobby. It was late in the afternoon and they had taken care of their regular appointments. The receptionist looked up. "We have more drop offs!" she announced, smiling. She held up several envelopes.

More money, quickly counted. Dr. Jim laughed. "This is getting serious."

The receptionist continued, "We've had at least thirty phone calls, people wanting to know how they can help. People are really amazing, aren't they?"

CHAPTER TWENTY-SEVEN
COMING IN

Maybe I should have told the hospital to not let you into my room," Sid said.

Lieutenant Wexley, smartly dressed in uniform, stood at the foot of his bed. She was an older woman, her white hair cropped under her military cap.

"I'm going to be leaving here today or tomorrow anyway," he continued. "Don't need to hear anything you're saying."

Connie had introduced the V.A. officer to Sid and this meeting was not going well.

"Sid, you're not making any sense. They need to check your eye, you still have a concussion, and that cut on your face could get infected. Who's going to take care of you?"

"Been on my own a long time now."

"Staff Sergeant —" she began, but Sid quickly held up a hand.

"Don't you call me that, nobody called me that for a long time. Don't deserve it, and I ain't in the Corps anymore."

"All right, we'll respect your wishes, but this country owes you a great debt. Whether you like it or not." She drew herself up into a rigid-backed position but her voice was still soft.

"You saved a lot of men, and they never got the chance

to thank you. Their families never got the chance to thank you. That would have been important to them. But even more important, we lost you, and we shouldn't have. We're very sorry about that."

Sid looked away. "I wanted to be lost. Lousy war, nobody should have been there that day. We were ambushed, no warning, just walked into that little village thinking everything was OK. Then the bombs went off, we were getting shot at." He stopped for a second. "Lousy war," he repeated.

Connie knew she was about to experience something profound. She exchanged looks with Lieutenant Wexley, who came around Sid's bed.

"We have the reports," the officer said. "You had so much courage that day. Not very many men would have done what you did, have the strength to do what you did. You were there for your brothers in arms."

She knew from experience that Sid, the Marine Corps Staff Sergeant, was ready for somebody from the military to be there. She'd seen it before, older veterans with a lot of memories, nightmares, to get off their chests, maybe ready to talk, maybe ready to come in. All it took was patience, and she was a very patient woman.

"How did you get shot?"

Sid shook his head. "I'm not real sure, gotta be honest about that. They told me later there was so much adrenaline in my body, I could have been shot several times and might not have gone down. All I know is later I felt a lot of blood on my legs, then I collapsed. Evacuated to Germany. Some doctor there said I was lucky, if the bullet had hit me just a centimeter in either direction I would never have walked again."

"And after being discharged to the states, you were supposed to enter therapy at a V.A. Hospital, but instead...well...you left."

Sid nodded. "No use going to any trouble for me."

"You've been on the road ever since?"

"Tried to go home, Indiana, you know that's where I'm from. But wasn't the same. I dunno. Made sense to leave and not come back. Disappear. Exactly like it's gonna make sense for me to walk out of here and disappear again."

Connie reached over to touch his hand. "You know you can't do that, don't you?"

Sid shrugged. "I've been hurt worse than this and besides, I got no place to go."

"That's not completely true," the lieutenant spoke up. "We'll have housing for you, a nice apartment with everything you need. Your therapy, medical bills, all paid for. And a monthly pension. We'll take care of you, Sid."

Sid was shaking his head, adamant in his stubbornness.

Connie was not as patient as the lieutenant.

"Sid, your hitchhiking days are over. Your left eye is

badly damaged. You might not have any vision in it at all. And Ben? You can't take him on the road. A three-legged dog? Are you telling me you're going to just leave him? Trust somebody else to take care of him? Or —." She didn't need to tell him what she was thinking. *Put him down?*

Sid hung his head, his lips trembling. He was trying hard not to cry.

She had hurt him, and now she was trying just as hard not to cry as well. "I'm sorry, that was harsh. You didn't deserve that."

He hung his head and gulped, "No. I did. Ben, oh my good boy Ben." He began to cry.

Connie bit back tears. Even the officer was clearly moved.

"Can I ask a favor?" he whispered to Connie. "Can I see him?"

His request didn't surprise her.

CHAPTER TWENTY-EIGHT
BEN & SID

It was unusual, but the doctor and hospital staff saw no reason to refuse Sid's request. They had read the newspaper, too. Sid was a hero. How could they say no?

Connie called Dr. Sheila and told her what Sid wanted.

"That's a good idea," the veterinarian said. "We've been worried about Ben, he hasn't woken up yet and it's past time he should."

A few minutes later a van with the Veterans' Administration logo pulled up in front of the veterinary hospital. Sid was helped into a wheelchair, then Connie pushed him into Dr. Sheila's office and sat in a chair next to him.

Dr. Sheila was waiting for them. She knew Sid's face had been badly injured but she was still shocked to see so much of his face covered in gauze.

"I know you've heard this many times, we're sorry for what happened to you," she told him. "And Ryan, a terrible loss. Heart broke about Classy, too."

He nodded.

"Did Connie tell you what we had to do with Ben?" she asked. She dreaded this part of the conversation.

"You amputated one of his legs."

"We can show you the X-rays, the limb was badly crushed, the bones in splinters. We're always worried about infection with an injury like that. There was nothing we could do. It wasn't an easy decision to make. I hope you understand."

He held up his hand. "I appreciate what you did, have no problems with that. I know you save him. But, a three-legged dog. Is that, well, a good thing?"

Dr. Sheila leaned into her desk, arms folded. "It's not a great thing, I'll be honest with you, but it's a good thing since he's still alive. If you're asking how a dog with three legs gets around, the answer is remarkably well. Ben won't be able to jump or leap like before, obviously. He'll need help for some things like getting into a high truck, but he'll be able to walk, trot, even run. There are many videos on the Internet showing how well dogs adjust. I'll show them to you. They're sometimes called 'tripod' dogs, by the way.

"He'll need some therapy, get him used to his new life. And we'll watch for things like arthritis. He lost one of his front legs, so that will put stress on the other one. He's a big dog. Watching his weight will be important.

"But," she smiled, "he's young and that means he'll do just fine."

Sid nodded. "Connie said he hasn't woken up, yet."

"No, not yet, but hearing your voice might be the thing

he needs. Ready to see him?"

***

Ben was laying on a bed in the hospital's puppy playroom. The veterinarians thought it would be a better setting, informal and cozy. Sid's wheelchair was positioned as close to Ben as possible.

The big dog was prone, unmoving, his eyes closed. A tube protruded from his neck leading up a stand next to the bed.

Sid swallowed. It was hard seeing Ben like this He stroked the dog's long fur." It doesn't seem to be shining like it used to," he muttered.

"He's not getting the nutrition he needs in the I.V.," Dr. Jim explained. "It's enough to keep him going, of course, but it's not like the good diet he should be eating. Plus, he's been through a lot. Stress takes something out of a dog's body."

"His collar…"

"The clasp was cracked, it wouldn't stay fastened."

"Guess that's not important," he muttered, stroking Ben's back and fluffing his ears. "Hey, Ben, I'm here. It's ol' Sid. Remember me? I'm right here with you, just like always.

"I can't wait to feed you some pork chops, that was our first supper together. And macaroni and cheese. I know that's not the kind of thing I should be feedin' you so I hope you didn't tell these good doctors about that."

The veterinarians exchanged glances, appreciating the light moment but knowing how difficult this must be for Sid.

Sid kept talking, his voice cracking.

"Camping by the river. Hearing everybody who picked us up talking about their dogs.

"Remember when we saw those horses in the canyon? I don't think you'd ever seen a horse before, but you stayed right with me, didn't chase them or anything. That beautiful stallion just staring at us. It was something special, wasn't it?

"And you helped that mama after she crashed her car. You know if it wasn't for you, who knows what could have happened to her little baby? I knew what you was thinking, you knew what I was thinking. You and me, we made a great team that day. It seems so long ago…"

There was still no response from Ben. Connie reached out to touch Sid's shoulder. Maybe this wasn't such a good idea. She swallowed hard. It was difficult watching Sid's emotions crumble in front of her. This brave man, a hero many years ago, a hero yet again, so attached to his dog. Listening to him recount the many adventures they'd had together, some wonderful, some with obvious danger, was breaking her heart.

Sid stroked Ben's head, his fingers massaging the dog's nose and behind his ears. "Ben, you saved my life, didn't you, the other night. You hurt the guy who was hurting me, got him off of me. He had that knife, but you just plowed right into him. He didn't expect that. Well, I didn't either.

"Come back, will you? I'm going to be facing a lot of changes, and you know how I hate changes. I really don't think I can do this without you. I need you. Please. I love you more than I've loved just about anybody in my life."

What else could he say? Overcome, he put his head down between Ben's paws. His hands clutched Ben's fur as though they would never let go.

***

Ben saw the blackness getting less black, but he fought it. He was getting pretty comfortable in it. Lazy, actually. Nothing to think about. Nothing to feel. Nothing to hurt him. Nothing to eat.

OK, that part was kind of bad. At the end of the day, no matter what had happened, he *liked* eating.

The delicious smell of pork chops was luring him out of the blackness.

Wait.

Was that's Sid's voice? Yes, it was Sid, but he could barely make out what he was saying. Sid wasn't in the blackness, he was above it. A long way above it. Ben remembered the river, the horses, the Baybee.

Ben concentrated, imagined himself on a hill, looking out

over a canyon. He'd been exploring, climbing and jumping over rocks and ledges. The sun on his body. A cool breeze dancing in his eyes. Sid calling, "Good boy, Ben!"

With a start, he realized he hadn't imagined the hill, or the canyon, or Sid calling to him.

It had really happened.

I have never been so happy in my life.

***

Was there a subtle shift in the light of the room? A glimmering ray of sun, perhaps? A warm breeze that might have come from an open window? But this room had no windows to see any sunshine or feel fresh air from outside.

The flicker of a small strand of fur on Ben's head, almost unnoticed.

Almost.

Dr. Sheila reached out to her husband's arm. He had seen it, too.

Another flicker, now on his neck, caused her to gasp.

"Keep talking to him, Sid," she whispered. Nobody wanted to move and everybody wanted to believe.

The lump in Sid's throat was making it almost impossible to speak. "You're still in there, Ben, you gotta be." He lifted his head. "Please wake up. I need you. You're my good boy Ben."

***

Three Magic Words.

***

Sid put his head back down, ready to give up on Ben, on himself.

Until he looked up, and through his tears, saw a pair of amber eyes watching him.

CHAPTER TWENTY-NINE
TRIPOD

Every day the newspaper gave its readers updates on the "Ripper's Raid" as it was now being called.

FOUR ARRESTED, TWO STILL IN HOSPITAL
HERO DOG LOSES LEG
HERO OWNER MIGHT LOSE EYE
"WE WON'T TOLERATE
THIS KIND OF THING
IN OUR TOWN" MAYOR SAYS
SHERIFF SAYS PLANNED CLEAN-UP OF
LARGER CAMP POSTPONED

A subtitle headline was below:

RV Owner knows the hero who saved lives:
"Stops here every year, really great guy. And that
dog of his, he's a winner"

A local television station got an "exclusive" and a "leaked" segment of the Raiders' dashcam video, showing it on their various news shows for several days with the obligatory warning:

"This video is disturbing in nature, and should not be viewed by young children."

Each time the video ran, their ratings tripled; national news picked it up the next day.

***

Rex brought Brutus into the veterinary hospital on a leash.

Dr. Sheila looked up from her computer monitor and smiled. "You're looking good," she said to him.

"Got some bruises and my wrist is just about healed." He held up his left hand, still in a cast.

Rex thought it would be a good idea to get his dog's shots updated. He couldn't wait for the free clinics. He was making new plans for himself and Brutus.

Dr. Sheila took them into an examination room. The dog's temperature was taken, his ears and mouth checked, and his stomach and abdomen squeezed. A blood sample was taken; a heartworm check showed negative. Rex breathed a sigh of relief.

"He looks to be in pretty good shape," she said. Vaccinations were given and Rex was handed a year's supply of heartworm pills.

"I have a surprise for you," Dr. Sheila said, opening a

door to the hallway.

A minute later she led Sid and Ben into the exam room. "Sid's here visiting and watching Ben with his therapy."

Rex tried not to look too shocked at the bandage covering half of Sid's face, or the cautious way Ben was walking now that he had only three legs. "I thought you're still in the hospital."

"I am, they let me out to come over here to be with Ben," Sid answered.

They went outside, leading the dogs to sit in the shade.

"How's your eye?" Rex asked.

"Got another appointment with the doc tomorrow. I should know more by then."

"Ben looks good."

"It was touch and go after he got hurt. He only woke up a few days ago."

"Did they really have to take his leg off?" Rex asked.

"They showed me the x-rays." Sid nodded. "It was the best thing they could do. They call dogs missing a leg Tripod Dogs."

Rex leaned back and folded his arms. "Seems like they could come up with something better than that. Tripod Dog," he scoffed.

"He's able to walk pretty good. In a few months jog or trot. But," now it was Sid's turn to scoff. "We're grounded."

He told Rex about the apartment the V.A. was setting up

for him. "Haven't seen it yet, but they allow dogs. That had to be a condition. What about you?"

Rex cleared his throat. He gave Sid a side-ways glance. "I've been thinking about what you said, that day before the raid."

Sid tilted his head. "What was that?"

"Maybe for some of us, the camps ain't so good. I've always been kind of a loner so the small camps suited me, not a lot of people around, attracting attention."

"Cops say that raid was a bunch of guys bragging on the Internet…" Sid began.

Rex shook his head. "It can happen anywhere, any town. That proves it. Here's my plan. I figure I'll hit the road, like you did. Not stay in one place very long, don't get too comfortable. That's the key. Don't get too comfortable."

There was silence, Sid thinking about what he had just heard. "Guess I hadn't thought about it that way," he mumbled. *I just liked the road so that nobody would find out anything about me. And after I got Ben, so that nobody would find out anything about him, too.*

Rex stood up to leave.

"I hope you're landing in a good place, Sid," he said. "You probably saved my life, kept them from hurting me a lot more. Thank you for that. But I think I'm making the right decision.

"After all, maybe the world needs a Road Warrior to take

your place."

***

While their humans talked, Ben and Brutus caught up on what had happened to them.

"Have you seen Classy?" Ben asked.

Brutus shook his head. "Who? Oh yeah, Classy. Nope, but you know I forget a lot. So maybe I have."

"Where you staying now?" Ben figured he'd better ask more "today" kinds of questions.

"Some big building but Rex doesn't like it. I think we're getting ready to leave. What about you? You staying here?"

Ben shook his head. "I hope not. I have to sit in a cage a lot of the time and wait. Wait for somebody to take me for a walk, and it's not much of a walk, it's only outside through a door onto a tiny patch of grass for me to do my thing and I'm never left alone and somebody's watching me ALL THE TIME. A guy needs privacy sometimes.

"And then they do things to me and that's no picnic either, I'll tell you right now. They think it feels good massaging my chest, and well, it kind of does but they go on forever with it, you know? A few minutes is fine, but an hour? And then they're always trying to get me to stand up but something's not right and I have no idea what it is."

Ben gave out a big sigh. "I fall a lot."

You also complain a lot, Brutus thought but didn't say it out loud. He bent his head to get a closer look at Ben's chest.

"You only have three legs now. See?" he held up one of his paws. "Count them. I have four. You have three. That's why you keep falling."

Ben looked down at his chest. Yes, he'd heard this before, but it was hard to understand.

"I had four legs, once. Not that long ago, too."

"Well, pal, you don't now. Forget about what you used to have. Ain't important. Gotta be more like me. Forget it all."

Ben folded his ears back. "I like you, Brutus. You always tell a straight story, and you're diplomatic, too. You were a good friend to me and Classy. You might not remember, but I do. I'm sorry I'm complaining."

"That's OK. I sure hope things get better for you."

Rex pulled on Brutus' leash. They were getting ready to leave. "Maybe I'll see you around some time!" Brutus grinned.

"But, maybe not!"

CHAPTER THIRTY
A STRANGE QUESTION

Sid watched as Ben was hoisted above the floor, his three legs flailing about, trying to get good footing. The dog was fitted into a harness that cushioned his body with padded protection for the incision across his chest.

Ben grunted as the hoist was lowered into the warm water of the therapy pool. "This will help build up his strength and give him confidence," Dr. Jim said.

The harness was removed and Ben turned around. Like most dogs, he liked water anyway and was soon walking back and forth, enjoying the warmth.

Sid reached out to pet him. They were next to the surgery room in case one of Ben's incisions ruptured.

"He's doing really good." Dr. Sheila had been watching from the door, pleased at Ben's reaction to the water.

It had been more than a week since the attack on the homeless camp. Sid was transferred to the Veteran's Hospital where an ophthalmologist examined him. He was told some of the nerves might "reconnect" but he would probably only have about sixty percent of the vision in his damaged eye.

His headaches diminishing, he was allowed to take the

V.A. shuttle to the veterinarian's hospital where he spent two or three hours a day with Ben, sitting and talking to the dog. That time meant a lot to both of them.

"When are you going to be moving into your new apartment?" Dr. Jim asked. Connie had kept them up to date on the plans being made for Sid.

"Next week. They're buying me new clothes and furniture with all that money people donated." Sid looked down, suddenly embarrassed. "Can't thank people enough but they really shouldn't have." The "Sid and Ben Fund" had grown to more than fourteen thousand dollars, with more trickling in every few days.

"I think people are ashamed." Dr. Sheila shook her head. "That something like this could happen in our town, it woke a lot of folks up. You touched a lot of people's hearts."

Sid sniffed. "Ben did. I'm just the guy he was with."

He straightened up. "Do you think Ben'll be ready to come home with me when I move in?" Ben stopped himself in the water and looked at Sid, almost as though he was wondering the same thing.

Dr. Sheila smiled. "I think he's ready now. The two of you will be together again real soon.

"But," she held up a finger, "no macaroni and cheese, agreed?"

***

Lieutenant Wexley greeted him when he stepped down from the V.A. shuttle. She used a key to open the front door of his new apartment.

"Tell me what you think," she said. "If you don't like it, we'll change it, or find you another place."

Sid followed her in. New carpet, lots of windows which was good. A living room with plush new furniture including a recliner. On the opposite wall was a large rectangular TV.

She handed him the remote. "There are instructions on the end table."

Sid chuckled. "I'll need those, I have no idea how to work one of these things."

The living room blended into a kitchen with everything he could possibly use. New dishes, cookware, and cutlery. Dried flowers in a large basket were on a countertop to dress the place up.

One bedroom had a brand-new queen-sized bed with a matching dresser holding an assortment of clothes. A small lamp was on a night stand.

In the closet were several shirts and two new pairs of shoes, one for dress, the other casual.

A wide door led to a bathroom with a large walk-in shower. On the countertop next to the sink was a box with new bandages, gauze, and ointment for his face. He would have to change the dressing himself for the next few days but the doctor assured him he would soon be rid of all that.

The wound on his face was already beginning to itch, meaning it was healing, albeit slowly.

Another bedroom, smaller, was empty. "You can use this for whatever, maybe storage or just leave it as is. Entirely up to you to figure out," she told him.

They returned to the living room. She showed him the digital controls for the furnace and air conditioner. "Just push the buttons up or down, warmer or colder.

"Two more things," she said, reaching into her bag. "You have a debit card. You have money now, you can buy things. You'll be getting your monthly disability check deposited, too. And," she pulled out a small brightly-colored box, "here's your new phone."

Sid shook his head. "Do I have to?"

"Yes. For emergencies if nothing else. Not just for you. But for Ben, too."

He took the box and opened it.

"It's charged and there are already four numbers in it. The V.A. shuttle. Mine. Connie's. And Dr. Sheila's." She headed for the door, it was best to leave him alone sooner than later to get adjusted to his new life.

"Who knows? You might think of somebody you'd like to call. Stranger things have happened, right?"

***

There's adjusting, and then there's adjusting.

The first night Sid slept on the big bed. He should have been exhausted, but his mind wasn't, playing over and over the events of the last few days.

One thing nagged at him and it wouldn't go away.

Ben.

Everybody assumed he and Ben had been together a long time, maybe since he was a puppy. He hadn't told anybody otherwise, so why wouldn't they think that.

He ticked off on his finger the days they'd been together. A scarce three weeks, and many days of that were after the attack.

Sid had never lied to anybody about anything. Sure, he hadn't opened himself up like some people do, going on about their past and troubles and what not. That wasn't lying. That was just not talking.

Had it been a lie to not tell everybody about him and Ben? Or was that just not talking, too?

He knew the problem. He was suddenly surrounded by people in *authority*. People with *contacts*. People with *resources*. If they knew the truth, would they move heaven and earth to find Ben's real owner? How absolutely certain was he that Ben had been abandoned?

"It happens more than you want to think," was what Tess had said. Maybe the dog had just got lost? But nobody had called that local animal shelter, nobody had put up posters.

Tess had checked the Internet several times before they left. Nothing.

Had Sid decided to leave early because of Ben? Admit it to yourself, he thought. Deep down, even after only a couple of days, he didn't want to find Ben's owner, didn't want to lose the dog. He could have waited another week, maybe even two, before heading south. Why didn't he? More cobwebs messed with his mind, muddling his thinking.

Because he **wanted** to believe that Ben had been abandoned. Left in the middle of nowhere by a scum owner. Wearing only that collar, no tags...no...

The cobwebs cleared. Sid sat up and got out of bed.

He knew why his mind would not let this go.

***

The next day, Dr. Sheila's car pulled to the curb. Dr. Jim got out, the back door opened, and there was Ben.

Sid knelt and opened his arms to the big dog to hug him. Tail wagging like it would never stop, Ben returned the hug by resting his head on Sid's shoulder.

"You're home now, boy, you're home now," Sid said over and over.

The veterinarians hauled in several boxes and an extra-large bag of special dog food. "High-protein, which is what Ben needs," Dr. Sheila told Sid. They sat it down in the kitchen next to two shiny metal bowls for kibble and water. The bowls were set into a special wooden tray a foot above the floor. "He won't have to bend down to eat and drink," was the explanation.

There were also several packages of treats, a large dog bed, a new leash — and a new collar with a metal plate on it that read: Good Boy Ben.

Sid took it and smiled. "Perfect." He rotated the collar, heard the jangle of tags. Two of them, one for rabies the other a county license. He snapped the collar on the dog's neck. "Ben is legal, now." Everybody laughed.

Ben lapped up the attention, knowing they were talking about him.

"Uhm, say, this might seem like a strange question." Sid patted Ben on the head, then sat down in the recliner and leaned back, trying to look and sound casual. His stomach churned but he had to ask, had to hear the answer.

"I read a while back that some dogs have these things, microchips, in them. Did you by chance put one in Ben, you know, just for extra, uhm, protection and all?"

"Oh!" Dr. Sheila exclaimed. "I almost forgot to tell you. We assumed you'd never had that done, but you were still in the hospital, pretty much out of it after your surgery, we couldn't ask. But we checked just to make sure. Don't want to have two of these things in a dog, messing up the scanning process. Of course, we didn't find one, you know that, so he's got one now, right in his neck. You can't even see where it goes in."

Sid blinked and tried not to sigh too audibly. "You thought of everything."

"Here's some pain medication, but he might not need it." Dr. Sheila handed him a small bottle of capsules. "Don't give it to him unless you think he's hurting.

"Try to keep him calm if you can. That might be hard, but we don't want him too excited, no jumping around. We'd like to continue water therapy three times a week, maybe for the next month, if that's all right with you. On the other days, you can take him for a short walk, ten minutes to start then work up to longer. If he looks like he's getting tired, head back right away, but I know you won't let that happen. You'll do a good job watching him."

"Slow and steady," Sid agreed. "We can do that, right, Ben?" The dog looked up at him and seemed to agree.

***

They watched TV together, Ben staying close to Sid's chair. Ben tried to scratch an ear with a rear leg. He was unstable and almost fell over. Sid rose to help, but Ben righted himself with a look that seemed to say, "I'm OK, no worries." Sid nodded and returned to his chair.

Supper was soup and salad for Sid, kibble for Ben.

Sid moved the dog bed into his bedroom. Ben couldn't jump on the bed to sleep with him, but hopefully that would come later.

Ben curled up on his bed, but didn't go to sleep right away. He got up several times. Sid heard him move around in the house before returning to his bed, but within a few minutes getting back up again.

Sid couldn't sleep, either, so he went to look for Ben.

He found him in the living room, sitting and staring out the window.

"Can't sleep?" Sid asked, sitting down in a chair next to him. "Strange place, isn't it."

They watched out the window, the dark shapes of the houses across the street, an occasional passing car, headlights gleaming on the pavement.

Neither of them went back to bed that night.

***

This looks familiar, Ben thought. Houses and a road. A window to look out from. Familiar, but not the same.

I wonder if we're going to leave soon. Get more rides in cars. Where's the tent we used to sleep in?

He glanced at Sid, wishing and hoping the human could read his thoughts, understand his questions, and had answers.

***

Sid had an idea and called for the V.A. shuttle the next morning.

Ben was dropped off at the veterinarian for his daily therapy and Sid asked the driver to take him downtown. An hour later he was back at his apartment with several boxes.

The driver helped Sid carry them in. "Need some help with these?" he asked, more than a little curious. He had seen what the boxes held.

"Nope," Sid answered. "But thanks, anyway. This'll give me something to do today."

The driver left, and Sid carried the boxes into the spare bedroom. Sid had "figured out" what to put in there.

THIRTY-ONE
OLD HABITS

Lieutenant Wexley arranged to pick up Ben that day and bring him home after his therapy. She had some formal papers for him to sign, and this would give her an excuse to check on him. She didn't want to intrude but she knew from experience that Sid might be having trouble adjusting to his new life.

She had seen regression before. It was hard for some homeless people to come in off the streets. They had friends, carving out a lifestyle that seemed odd for many, but workable for them. Would Sid go back to his old life, too, despite the injury to his eye? Despite Ben's handicap?

She stopped and got take-out. Food always helped to open doors. The dog picked up the delicious aromas and he made like he was going to climb into the front seat.

"Not for you big boy," the lieutenant smiled. "You're on a doggy diet. No more catch as catch can like you're used to."

At the apartment, she helped Ben from the back seat of her car. Sid was waiting for them at the door and helped her with the bags of food.

"Dr. Sheila says he's doing great," she told him. "He jumps right into that therapy pool."

She pulled down plates and glasses from the kitchen

cupboards. This gave her the chance to look around. If a previously homeless person was having problems, she would see it immediately. Dishes piled up in a sink, clothes strewn about, an empty refrigerator, dust on tables.

Sid's apartment was still clean, dishes arranged neatly, nothing in the sink, the countertop gleaming. She peeked into his bedroom. Bed made, no clothes on the floor.

The door to the smaller bedroom was closed, it would probably stay empty.

She went back to the living room. The end table next to the recliner had several books. Sid saw her looking at them.

"I lost my books in the raid. Ben and I've been exploring the neighborhood a little on our walks. There's a used book store nearby."

She couldn't help but notice that two of the books were about dogs. She hid her smile.

"How you getting along with the TV? Got the remote figured out?"

"Kind of. I found lots of channels with nothing but music. I like those."

She returned to the kitchen to set the table. "I got Italian."

"Can I pay you for it? Seems I have money, now. Somebody told me I can buy things."

They laughed. "Nope," she told him. "It's on me, free."

"I won't pass up a free lunch." Sid smiled. "Old habits

die hard."

***

Later that night Sid went into the bathroom to change the bandage on his face. He carefully peeled the tape off, then pulled the gauze away from his face, looking at himself in the mirror the whole time to make sure it came away in one piece.

The left side of his face was now exposed. His eye was terribly bloodshot and he had to take care when he bandaged it to make sure the gauze didn't touch the more sensitive areas.

He twisted his head this way and that, inspecting his face. He would have to live with this scar for the rest of his life, a permanent reminder of what had happened that night. A permanent reminder of what had been lost.

Ben padded up to the door to look in on Sid.

"What do you think of my new look?" Sid asked him. "Dashing, mysterious, or will I frighten little children every time I go out?"

Ben tilted his head the way dogs do when they're trying to figure something out.

"I'm going to take that as dashing and mysterious," Sid smiled.

He began to cut the gauze he would need to cover the

wound, but looked at himself in the mirror again.

For the first time he wondered if the scar would be as noticeable if his skin was different.

If he had white skin.

If his black skin would make the scar more of a glaring gash.

He remembered all too clearly what Monkey Face had said when he held Sid by his arm. *"We not only got us a homeless dude, he's a —"*

How would he have finished that sentence if he'd had the chance? "He's a black man." Or use one of the more salacious slurs for the color of his skin?

Probably the slur.

Over the years on the road, he knew the few friends he had made were worried about him, maybe more worried about him because he was black. Tess came to mind. She had never talked to him directly, but he always sensed she would have liked to have seen him give up the hitchin', wishing he'd stay in one place. A place where he wouldn't be threatened. A safe place.

Well, he thought as he began to tape the new bandage on his face, s*he got her wish. Maybe he'd let her know sometime in the coming months. And let her know that staying in one place, a safe place, might not be such a bad thing.*

***

Ben was tired, maybe he would sleep better tonight. He hated to admit it, but being in that big tub of warm water was nice. His legs worked a lot better than on the floor and his paws (the ones he had left) didn't hurt. The water was relaxing, and it made him drowsy. When Ben said it was time for bed, he didn't balk.

Sid opened another door on the other side of the bedroom and Ben heard the click of the light. "Come on in here. This is where we're sleeping."

Ben glanced in, then looked at Sid with wide eyes.

There was a tent! That's amazing! He stepped inside. It was much bigger than the one they'd had before and took up most of the room. He could really stretch out!

The floor was different, too, not on hard ground but kind of soft and cushy. He heard Sid say, "Air mattress" *like I'm supposed to know what that is, but OK, I'll get on it.*

He found his footing, then waited for Sid to get in, too. He sighed, happy and grateful.

Somehow, Sid had heard him. Somehow, Sid had given him what he wanted.

***

Sid climbed in. "I'm having a hard time sleeping, too." He reached out to pull Ben a little closer.

"Maybe we'll get used to the regular bed. Eventually.

Perhaps you'll be able to jump on it. Eventually.

"But, you know better than I do. Old habits die hard."

CHAPTER THIRTY-TWO
ABOUT TWO MONTHS LATER

The dog park was busy, people taking advantage of the nice weather before winter set in. Big dogs, small dogs, playing together or sitting with owners.

Sid walked Ben back and forth along the fence on a leash near the entrance. Ben was sporting a bright blue bandana over his collar; the dog looked quite proud of it.

"He's doing pretty good!" Sid waved to his friends. Dr. Sheila, Dr. Jim, and Connie stood nearby. Dr. Sheila gave him a thumbs up.

"When did he finish his therapy?" Connie asked them.

"Several weeks ago," Dr. Jim answered, beaming. "He really doesn't need us anymore except for annual checkups. He's our star patient."

Connie changed the subject. "Are you going to have your mobile clinic available next year?"

Dr. Sheila nodded. "We hope so. We're applying for more grants, and Mr. and Mrs. Lee are keeping that location open. They said they won't lease it out so we can use it whenever we want."

Three weekends of the previous month had been busy ones for the local veterinarians. The community had responded very generously with free coffee, soft drinks, and sandwiches for the homeless people who brought their dogs. They also had plenty of volunteers who wanted to help.

The number of animals cared for was impressive: More than 400 dogs were examined and vaccinated with 330 spays and neuters. Several female dogs were already pregnant and couldn't be spayed, but at least they were identified and follow-ups were scheduled to take care of the puppies when they were born.

Just as important, many of the homeless — and some of the volunteers — found there was little to fear from each other.

The social worker had also been busy, finding housing for the raid's displaced campers. Most were in small apartments or community housing, but a few, like Rex and Brutus, had disappeared.

"What about the Rippers?" Dr. Sheila asked Connie.

"The trials will begin the first of next year," she answered. "Three of them face third degree murder charges, assault with a deadly weapon, as well as charges for vandalism, animal cruelty, public disturbance, and arson. They found the other one who helped plan it, he's facing accessory charges.

"I think they'll be put away for a very long time. The local media, and the community, are still very engaged in the tragedy, and I hope that lasts. People can be kind of fickle."

They watched as Sid brought Ben back to them.

"Not sure I feel good about letting him off leash," Sid told them.

"It should be OK," Dr. Sheila said. "The wound is completely closed up. Fur's even growing over it."

A young boy ran up to Sid, "My dad says you're a hero," he grinned, motioning over to an adult, who raised a hand in greeting. "This is a brand-new ball, for your dog. Can I give it to him?"

***

I'm a half-rememberin', half-forgettin' kind of dog, Ben reminded himself. *What do I remember, what do I forget?*

"I remember everything!" Classy's words suddenly came back to him, as though the little dog was right there, at his side. "Maybe that's good, maybe not, but I sure wish I could forget some things," he heard her say. "Maybe everything. Might make life easier."

Ben closed his eyes.

Forget.

And opened them to see a ball in Sid's hand.

***

Sid was about to tell the boy thanks, that Ben wasn't a fetchin' kind of dog. He made as if to give the ball back, when something told him to stop. Ben was looking at the ball in a different way, tail wagging.

Were those amber eyes gleaming?

Sid turned back to his new friends, to get their attention, as if to say, "Watch this."

He unclipped the leash.

He threw the ball. It arced in the air for only seconds, while the world stood still and watched.

***

Science tells us that light travels the fastest of anything in our universe. A Danish Astronomer, Ole Roemer, became the first person to measure it in 1676. It cannot be seen by the human eye.

But how can science (or Ole Roemer, if he was at the dog park that day) explain the explosion of the golden coat of a dog named Ben who broke free in a surge of joy and ran, ran, ran, as fast as he could. Faster than any beam of light could ever be measured.

***

Ben faltered on the slick grass. He heard people around him gasp. He got up, then stumbled again.

I have to get ahead of that ball!

He urged himself on. *Willed* himself on.

The space where his leg had been wasn't empty anymore. The bad memories, the ones he thought he would never forget? Gone, too.

He stumbled again. *Get up, get up, get up.*

The ball was just above him, a little red orb against the blue sky.

***

"Run faster, Ben, run faster!" he heard Sid shout, joy singing in his voice. "You can do it!" More people were shouting, cheering him on.

***

Ben looked down. *Oh! There's happy little Classy and she's running beside me, panting and laughing.* Her little legs weren't pounding the ground, they were catching the wind!

Come on, Ben, come on, she was telling him. *I'll lift you up, now! Jump with me!*

Ben turned his head to look back ever so slightly, and in a blur, heart pounding, the day filled with ecstasy, he leaped.

Ben.

      Caught.

           The.

                 Ball.

I have never been so happy in all of my life.

"Good Boy Ben!!!"

Three Magic Words.

READ ON FOR A PREVIEW OF
THE THIRD BOOK IN
THE ABANDONED SERIES

If you liked *Good Boy Ben*'s Tess and
her daughter, Becky, you'll love

AUTUMN AND THE
SILVER MOON STALLION
Coming in late 2023!

CHAPTER ONE
THE SILVER MOON

The filly backed out of the old horse trailer and down the sagging wooden ramp. The man led her several feet away and her halter was taken off. She shook her head. She had always worn these tight pieces of leather above her muzzle, and it was strange not feeling them bite into her flesh.

The man left her to walk back to the trailer. Her ears flicked in curiosity. The door was slammed with a loud. "Bam!"

The truck started, gears ground, and it pulled away. The trailer rattled and bounced over ruts and rocks.

Seconds later, she was alone.

Hmm, she thought. This is a strange field. No fences.

No gates. Lots of dirt and rocks. Her tail whisked back and forth and she stepped forward a few feet. She bent down to pull at a strand of wild grass. It was sweet, and tasted better than her usual feed. She saw another patch, and ate it, too.

Now she was thirsty and smelled water. Following the scent, it led her down a gentle slope to a river bank. She carefully stepped over and around small stones, then splayed her legs to bring her lips to the water, and drank deeply.

This water was good, fresh, and clean. Much better than the dirty, rancid water she was usually given.

Sated, she went back up the slope to search for more sweet grass. Dusk was settling in, she was outside, but she wasn't concerned. She was always outside at night, in a field with no shelter or covering, so this was normal for her. Better than normal. Now she was eating tasty grass with clean water nearby. *All in all*, she thought, *I'm in a pretty good place.*

***

A white stallion stood on a high ledge near a cliff. He didn't move, wanting to stay hidden while he watched the filly. He knew she was fresh from human hands, could smell them on her, and that meant she was new to the wild, not wise to the range.

He wondered if the human would return to put the halter back on, put her in the trailer, drive her away. Another reason to stay hidden, unnoticed, in case that happened.

He watched as she climbed the river bank, looking for

more grass to nibble. His eyes never left her.

She gave no indication that she sensed he was there.

Night fell, and the silver moon rose in the sky.

IN MEMORY

Warren Barnes May 19, 1951 - Feb. 27, 2021

ABOUT THE AUTHOR

V P Felmlee is a former newspaper reporter and editor. She has written extensively for several magazines and is a board member of Women Writing the West. Her writing has won several awards and her latest novel was a finalist for Southwest Writers 2022.

Her first book, of The Abandoned Trilogy, *The Amazing, Interesting, Dangerous, and Somewhat True Adventures of Prince Tadpole & Princess Clara* was published in late 2022. The third book in the series, *Autumn and the Silver Moon Stallion*, will be published in late 2023.

She lives in Grand Junction, Colorado, with her husband and an assortment of dogs, cats, and chickens.

vfauthor.com

224

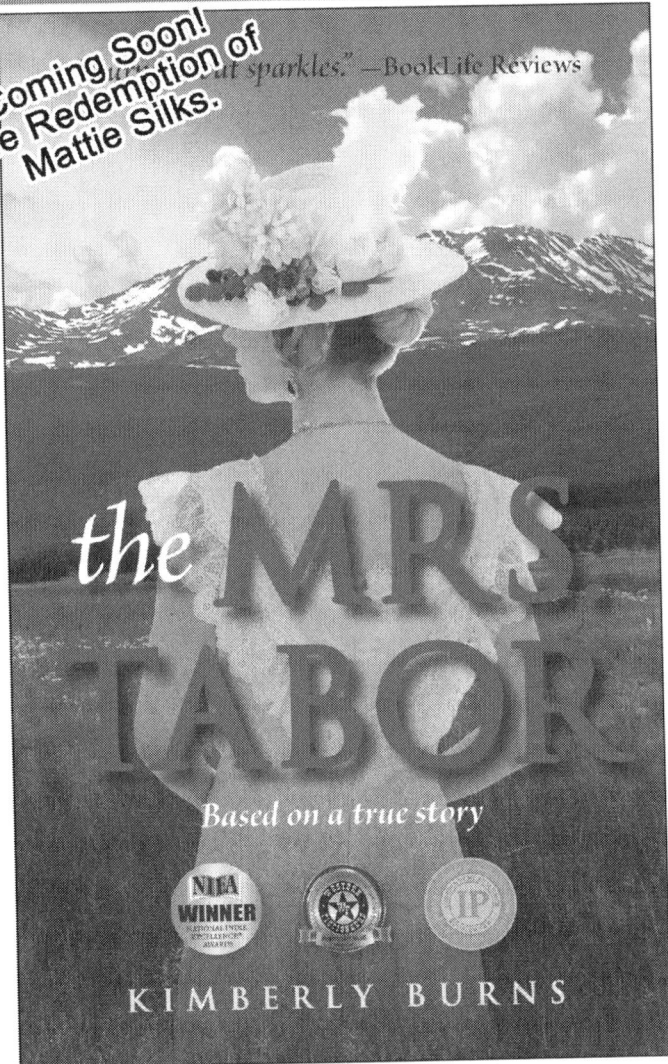

Coming Soon!
The Redemption of
Mattie Silks.

"...that sparkles." —BookLife Reviews

the MRS. TABOR

Based on a true story

KIMBERLY BURNS

kimberlyburnsauthor.com

2021 Gold Medal Winner Independent Publishers Awards,
Western Regional Fiction
2021 Winner National Indie Excellence Award, Regional Fiction: West
2021 Winner Western Fictioneers Peacemakers Award, Best First
Western Novel
2021 Finalist CIBA Laramie Book Awards for Best Americana &
Western Fiction
2021 Finalist Foreword INDIES Book of the Year

226

Made in the USA
Columbia, SC
18 August 2023

21727108R00130